A David

The Visitor's Choice

A Search to Make Things Right

Vinous,

Make Smart Choices!

Alexander Davidson

FERNE PRESS

Alexander Davidson

The Visitor's Choice: A Search to Make Things Right
Copyright © 2014 by Alexander Davidson

Layout, cover design, and illustratons by Jacqueline L. Challiss Hill
Cover photo by Alexander Davidson

Printed in the United States of America

Summary: When David Wilson finds himself in a foreign land, he discovers that his life is about to change dramatically.

Library of Congress Cataloging-in-Publication Data
Davidson, Alexander
The Visitor's Choice: A Search to Make Things Right/
Alexander Davidson–First Edition
ISBN-13: 978-1-938326-30-1
1. Fantasy. 2. Adventure. 3. Fiction. 4. Reading. 5. High school.
6. Middle school.
I. Davidson, Alexander II. Title
Library of Congress Control Number: 2014936363

FERNE PRESS

Ferne Press is an imprint of Nelson Publishing & Marketing
366 Welch Road, Northville, MI 48167
www.nelsonpublishingandmarketing.com
(248) 735-0418

Dedication

This book is dedicated to my parents and teachers who helped instill in me a great love for reading and writing early on.

I would like to thank several people who helped make this journey possible.

There would not be a book if my editor, Kris Yankee, and publisher, Marian Nelson, both of Nelson Publishing & Marketing, were not willing to take a risk on me and my manuscript. I am so grateful for my time spent talking about writing with Kris, since she brought out the best work I had in me.

I never would have even wanted to write a novel if it weren't for my parents, who read to me and made sure we always had shelves full of adventures. My teachers growing up were also crucial to fostering my love for reading and writing and to influencing my future career as an English teacher. These teachers include (but are not limited to) Mrs. Penny Carolin, Mrs. Connie Zbyrad, Mrs. Ellen Currier, and Mrs. Nancy Carapellotti.

It has been a long journey, and you can bet I talked about it to anyone who would listen. I would like to finally thank all my friends, family, and coworkers who have supported my dream, never doubted that it would come true, and never rolled their eyes whenever the topic came up in conversation. Thank you to those who were early readers and critics as well, including (but not limited to) Daniel Spilker, Amy Davidson, and Erin Williamson.

This journey has been amazing and it wouldn't have been the same without you, even if I forgot to mention you here.

Chapter One

"What the heck?!" David shouted, as he fell into midair. He caught himself on the arm of the sofa and clung for dear life.

Who dug a hole right in the middle of the library floor? he thought.

He kicked out his legs to see if he could find the bottom. He didn't find it. He kicked leaves and wood instead. David looked around.

What? How did a tree get here?

He tried stepping on the branch to climb back to the safety of the couch that happened to be in a tree, but the branch broke beneath his weight. The sudden jolt caused his fingers to slip a little bit.

"No. No. No. Please no," he begged.

David tried to pull himself back up, but he was losing his grip.

"Help!" David screamed. "Is anybody there?"

He tried a second time to rise up back to safety, and his arms gave out. He was falling. Instinctively, David swung his arms out to catch himself, but his hands slid off the smooth fabric and down he fell.

David's fall was not a smooth one. As he fell, he got smacked, scratched, and beaten up the whole trip down by he didn't know what.

David's life didn't flash before his eyes. All he could see was the grass below grow closer and closer. He tried reaching out for anything to grab onto but only got handfuls of leaves in return. David could see the features of the ground floor get clearer and clearer until—*slam!*—David crash-landed into a coffee table. In case you are wondering, coffee tables are not the most comfortable objects to break your fall.

With the wind knocked out of him, David focused his attention on gulping precious air instead of on the details of this very unusual situation. Gradually, as more oxygen traveled to his brain, he could think again. He tilted his head from side to side, noticing some of his surroundings.

David observed more of his current environment. He saw grass, trees, and leaves. *Did I just smash into a coffee table in the middle of a forest?*

"What on earth is going on?" David said to himself.

On his back with pieces of shattered wood underneath him, David looked up at the tree he had recently exited.

"Is that Mr. Linden's couch?" David knew couches didn't belong in trees, but there it was.

David gently sat up and put his hand to his head. His head stung where he touched. David let out a surprised yelp. *Did I injure myself in the fall?* For some reason, he felt that the bump on his head must have come from something else. But just what, David couldn't remember.

Taking in his surroundings, David found himself in a clearing surrounded by a dense wall of trees. He looked at the handful of leaves, and he felt the wet, spiky grass beneath his feet. Slowly, a thought formed in his mind. He shook it away, but it re-formed even faster. Eventually, he just had to say it.

"I don't think I'm in Mr. Linden's library anymore."

Was this a prank?

"Hello?" David called out. "Mr. Linden?"

He looked around, but there was no response. Mr. Linden wouldn't have moved a sleeping boy into the middle of a forest and up into a tree. Granted, Mr. Linden did have a reputation for having weird habits, and David honestly didn't know him that well yet, but he could feel this wasn't something that man would do.

Maybe his school friends? It had to be.

"Guys?" David tried again. "Okay, you had your fun. You can come out now."

David didn't think falling out of a tree was really that fun, but it was the type of prank his friends would pull on him for abandoning them this summer to stay with Mr. Linden instead of lounging by the pool, riding bikes to the movies, or playing summer league lacrosse. "I'm the one who was abandoned, not you," he muttered.

"Guys?" he said louder.

Still no answer.

David got to his feet and studied the large tree in front of him. He circled it to get a better view. He looked at the intricate branches of the old wooden beast. David liked his friends, but he admitted, "There is no way they could have pulled this off."

Instead of spending too much time imagining how a bunch of high school students could manage to get a couch and a boy out of a house, into the woods, and up into a tree without that boy waking up, David decided he needed to shift his focus to more pressing matters. First, he was still in his T-shirt and pajama pants that he went to bed in last night. The crisp morning dew on his bare feet was starting to feel uncomfortable. Second, he needed to figure out where he was. Most likely he was still somewhere on the grounds of Mr. Linden's estate, but David had not yet gone exploring. The only way to find out was to start walking. *But which way?*

David scanned the wall of trees around him hoping to find traces of the roof or a chimney from Mr. Linden's mansion or at least find the hints of a trail. No luck. While circling the clearing, David forgot to look where he was going and stepped on a jagged piece of what used to be a table.

"Ouch," he yelled.

David jumped back, slipped on the wet grass, and fell back onto the pile of broken wood a second time.

"Twice in one day!"

Someone giggled nearby. David sat up quickly and spun his head around in all directions. "Hello?" More giggling. "Is someone there?" he called out. The giggling was coming from another direction now. "I have a weapon."

"No, you don't," a small voice said.

David turned around again and saw a young girl leaning against a tree, her long hair in braided pigtails pouring over her shoulders. She was short and skinny, but also slightly rough and tan. She was a little girl, make no mistake, but David had the feeling this tomboy wearing a shirt and ripped shorts could definitely prove her worth if the time came.

She spoke again. "I checked you while you were sleeping. You have nothing on you. Nothing of value anyway."

David felt silly to still be wearing his pajamas.

"Who are you?" he asked. "Where am I?"

"You don't know where you are? These are the woods of Ethelrod. Don't you recognize them?"

Ethelrod? David was admittedly new to the area, but he had never heard of such a place. Then again, maybe there were forests all over that had official names he never knew of or cared to read about.

"Look, do you know a Mr. Linden? Can you tell me how to get back to his place?" David asked.

"I don't know who that is," she replied.

This was frustrating. He tried an easier question, silly as it sounded in his head. "Can you at least confirm I'm still in Michigan?" That question should be a no-brainer for a little girl.

She stared blankly. "What's a Michigan?" Looks like it wasn't that simple after all.

"A state…" The girl showed no recognition. "In the United States of America…" Nothing. "Okay, what did you say this place was called again?"

"Ethelrod," she answered. David could see a slight change coming over the girl's face. "Haven't you ever heard of it?"

"Of course not," David said. Ethelrod? Was there really such a place? If it was local, he'd never heard of it. If it was a city or a country, the same applied. Was this a place he should know about? Maybe if David had read more, he might have heard about it. What kind of name was Ethelrod? "Where am I? What is Ethelrod? Who are you?" he asked again.

"Then…then you are a visitor." Her body seemed to tense. "Quick, what is your name?"

"Hold on. I asked you first. Tell me your name," David demanded.

"My name is Gretchen," she answered. "Are you a visitor?" Gretchen inched backward with slow footsteps. "I've been told all visitors are hurtful and should not be trusted."

David gave in. "Well, I am a visitor, but I promise I won't hurt you. I have no idea where I am. My name is David."

She relaxed. "Well, David, we need to get you to the king. All visitors must see the king, but I'll admit we haven't had any visitors to these parts for quite some time. And the country is not very welcoming to them."

King? Country? If this was still part of a childish prank, it had gone on long enough. What were the odds that his friends had knocked him on the head and transported him on some cargo plane to another location? It would explain the bump on his head, but no way. His friends weren't that good. Or that rich. This girl obviously had to have something wrong with her. He needed to leave now and find his way back.

"To the king?" David questioned. "I'm not seeing any king. I need to get home. Now."

"But you must!" Gretchen exclaimed. "It's a custom. Just come with me, and everything will be fine."

"Yeah, that doesn't sound like something I'm going to do."

"We aren't allowed to just let visitors to Ethelrod wander around. If we find one, it is the law in this land to bring them straight to the king. Come on, let's go." For a little girl, she was pretty sure of herself. She had no problem telling a boy clearly almost more than a decade older than she was what to do.

"The law of the land? I am not from this land," David debated. "I'm not even sure I believe you. I'm still in Mr. Linden's backyard somewhere. I have to be. And I am going to find my way back, with or without your help."

"But in Ethelrod—" she started.

David interrupted. "There is no such place as Ethelrod! I'm going home."

David turned and walked away quickly into the thickness of the woods, leaving the little delusional girl behind him.

Chapter Two

David fought through strong branches and kicked his way past thick undergrowth. He didn't know where he was going, but it had to be better than following a little girl into the hands of a king who ruled a country with a crazy made-up name that hated visitors. No, thank you.

David tried to follow a straight line. Eventually he would hit the end of the forest or a road or something that would help him find his way. What he did find, however, was not as useful. Unsure of the sound, David walked toward what he thought was a highway, only to find a vast and thundering river. There was no way across, and it looked like the river went on for miles.

Even though David didn't grow up living near Mr. Linden, he was positive there weren't any rivers like this in the area. Well, he was pretty sure. Was he sure? If only he had actually read his geography book, he might have known more that could tell him where he was and how to get back. Maybe that textbook was more useful than he originally thought, but in his defense, that class was unbearable.

Only a week ago, before waking up in the middle of the woods, David had been sitting in class, bored out of his mind. Ticking off minutes in his notebook wasn't the most stimulating activity David could think of, but it was better than what everyone else was doing. While the teacher wrote notes on the board, the students were asked to read from their required novels. David hated reading. He thought that watching the clock and adding dashes to the margin of his notebook would be a much better use of his time.

David crossed out the number five. Five minutes left in class.

He didn't dislike others who read. He didn't have a problem with that; reading just wasn't for him. Why should he read two or three hundred pages to learn a lesson the teacher would just tell him later in class? Why put in all of that extra effort when there were more important things to worry about, like keeping his A in chemistry or the upcoming lacrosse playoffs?

David crossed out the number four. Four minutes left in class.

David preferred television and video games, where the action and characters were right there on the screen in front of him. When he read books, they were just black and white symbols on pages. Words didn't really mean much to him. He couldn't follow along with the books his teachers chose and was never able to visualize the setting or the characters, which made it even harder to figure out who was who and what was happening. It was a struggle for something that wasn't even really worth it in the long run. Boring.

David crossed out three. Three minutes.

David had more important things to do, like count down the minutes until the end of class. Then he would be free from the school day, and he could do what he wanted. And in just a few more days, it would be summer vacation, when David wouldn't be expected to read or think for a few months.

Two. Two minutes.

Finally, the bell rang and students packed the halls, eager to be anywhere but there. David was almost trampled by a group sprinting out of the biology lab where a stink bomb had just gone off. He politely held the door open for a female teacher and continued to hold it open for another soul in need, a student carrying a pile of books and crumpled papers who was whispering frantically to himself, worried about the upcoming finals. David just shook his head at the poor fellow putting forth so much time and effort, preparing for a few short hours of his life. David wasn't a lazy kid; things just came more easily to him so he was able to work less and focus on the things he actually wanted to do instead. This did not include rereading chapters upon chapters of uninteresting texts for school.

"Hey, Dave! Wait up!" Paul ran through the crowd. David noticed that Paul had fallen asleep in the last class and missed the bell. David had wondered whether or not his friend would make it to the bus on time. "Do you have a geography textbook I can borrow?"

"Yeah, sure," David replied. "Come with me to my locker to get it."

Paul followed. "You sure you don't need it? It's the first final this week."

"No, I haven't used that thing all year." Paul looked at David in disbelief. David explained, "Everything we need to know is from class. As long as I take notes, pay attention, and ask questions, I can get away perfectly fine without ever opening the darn thing."

"But what about all of the applications and stuff for the exam?" Paul asked.

"I'll figure something out. I always do," David said. "I get good grades, so why spend more time reading? What good has that ever done me?"

Paul shrugged. "I guess you're right. You have better grades, so something must be working."

They reached David's locker, and David put in his combination. Paul asked, "What about English class? What about all those novels? Some of them were pretty good."

David joked, "Yeah, I liked their summaries online." Paul laughed. "But let's be honest, when am I ever going to have a conversation about Charles Dickens or Jane Austen these days? Give me math and science, stuff I can actually use."

David took out his hardcover geography textbook, whose spine had never been broken, and handed it to Paul. "Keep it. I can make it the last few days without working on my mapping skills."

Boy, was David wrong about that. Having at least some knowledge about major rivers in the area would come in handy right about now. Maybe walking in a different direction would do the trick.

Making sure he wasn't going directly back the way he came, David picked a different direction and started walking. Without being able to completely see the sky through the trees, he wasn't absolutely sure which way he was going.

Dad gave me a survival guide book of crazy situations for my birthday one year, David remembered. *It seemed worthless at the time. Maybe I should've read it. I bet I could use something from there now.*

Even though it probably had nothing to offer about falling asleep in a library and waking up in a new country, it might have had something to say about walking around the woods.

David continued walking and reached a clearing. His stomach dropped. His mouth was open wide in disbelief. There, in the middle of the clearing, was Gretchen. She was sprawled out on the grass, relaxing with her arms behind her head. She was wearing a circle of wild flowers in her hair, something she must have made to pass the time while David was away.

"How did you—" David began. "How did I—"

Gretchen got up. "There is only one path through the woods of Ethelrod, and there is no way you can find it without me."

"I can and I will," David protested. Gretchen pointed to the couch in the tree that clearly proved David had walked in a complete circle through the forest. David stared at the couch and then conceded, "Okay, okay."

Gretchen smiled. "I've been thinking. The only person who would know how to get you back home would be the king. And since the king doesn't even like visitors anyway, I'm sure he could help you get back."

David tried to think of any other option but was unable to. "How do I get there?" he asked. He was willing to play along for now. He hoped she could just lead him out of these woods and he would be able to get home from there.

"Lucky for you, I'm on my way to give something I found to him. Just another custom. You can come with me if you want." She pulled a satchel up over her head and onto her shoulder.

"Thanks, Gretchen." David agreed.

"Be sure to keep up, visitor!"

Chapter Three

There was no exact trail and yet Gretchen seemed to know exactly where she was going.

"Are we almost there?" David asked.

"We have a ways to go before we get out of these woods," Gretchen told him. "You just have to be patient and trust me."

"For a little girl, how do you know so much about this forest?"

"I have lived in Ethelrod my whole life. I like the woods. I like them better than fishing, anyway. My father is a fisherman. He always comes home smelly. The woods are better. And in the trees, I can be anyone or anything I want to be." David thought that sounded nice.

"Where do you live?" Gretchen asked.

"Well, right now I'm spending the summer with my Uncle Tom," he replied.

"The Mr. Linden you mentioned?"

"That's him. Well, he's more of a family friend," David said. "We aren't even related. It's just easier to say 'uncle' instead of explaining our weird relationship. I don't even know how my parents met him. They still call him my Uncle Tom, even though neither I nor my parents have seen him in years."

"But you are spending the season with him now."

"Yeah, my parents sent me to live with him. All of my friends are jealous. Mr. Linden has a reputation of being mysterious and extravagant, but who knows what he's been doing shut up in that big lonely house of his."

"Lonely?"

"Big fences, no visitors, no wife, no girlfriend. He doesn't even go into town. He has his groceries delivered."

"It sounds like your parents are sending you someplace good, though. It must be a pretty nice house if he never wants to leave it," Gretchen reasoned.

"Not as nice as where they're going," David added.

"What do you mean?"

"My parents are ditching me for some tropical couples retreat. I'll be taking care of myself again this summer. It's okay, though, I'm getting used to it. Over the past year, I've watched my parents and their relationship gradually unravel. Any time they were in the same room together, they were fighting. Fights usually involved me and my future, which in the beginning made me feel guilty. I eventually realized that they were actually fighting about something more though. The fights were getting pretty bad, so I'm happy to see them go on this retreat, even if I did see that their hotel reservation involved separate rooms."

Why am I opening up like this to a total stranger? David thought. He wasn't sure, but it felt good to say things he hadn't even talked about with his school friends.

David continued. "If my parents aren't fighting, they are barely speaking. That isn't much better for me. No communication means no coordinating driving schedules or dinner plans. This past season, I've grown used to finding rides home from lacrosse practice or games." David even learned how to cook from videos online after too many microwave meals to count.

"It sounds like you have a lot of responsibilities," Gretchen commented.

"At home, I'm only responsible for myself, but I'm good at it. This summer will not be a whole lot different than before. My friends are too far away to hang out with, and Mr. Linden, even with all his money, doesn't believe in owning a TV. Another summer on my own taking care of myself."

Another boring, regular summer for David.

At least, that's how it started. One night at Mr. Linden's, and now David was walking through trees following a little girl who believed they were in a make-believe country. At least this little mishap was shaking things up a bit.

Chapter Four

After David and Gretchen had walked for about an hour, the woods opened to a large field. On the other side of the field, David could see a medieval-looking town with a very large stone building in the center that he could only assume was where the king lived. David blinked and blinked again.

"Is that a—" he could hardly finish his sentence. "Is that a castle?"

"That, David," Gretchen said, "is the high kingdom of Ethelrod. I told you I wasn't making it up."

His head started spinning and he couldn't control his breathing. He turned away from Gretchen and threw up. Gretchen gave him a leather pouch of water from her bag, and he could stand straight again.

"A castle? Ethelrod?"

There was no way anything like this medieval town could have existed without people knowing about it. Was it all true? Was he really in a place called Ethelrod? It couldn't be. How did he get here?

Gretchen caught him before he completely collapsed on the ground.

"You really aren't from here, are you?" she asked.

"I'm really not."

"Then, let's see about getting you home."

"I would like that a lot," David replied.

They crossed the field of tall grass and wildflowers like the ones

Gretchen had in her hair. Eventually they made their way to the streets of the town that were filled with people going in and out of shops. Even more shopping and trading spilled over to carts in the streets. Gretchen walked proudly through the street as if nothing were different, and yet everyone else stopped what they were doing and stared.

David could feel their attention on him, probably because he was in public in his pajamas in the middle of the day. But these people weren't wearing clothes that were all too normal either. No jeans, no sneakers, no T-shirts. Everyone looked like they were out of place and out of time. Had David come across some type of Renaissance fair? That sure would make up for the fact that he was seeing horses instead of cars and shops for cobblers instead of electronics. In fact, no one seemed to have any electronics. David couldn't even find a Renaissance worker sneaking music through a strategically placed earbud snaking down to an MP3 player. No one was even texting in the back corner. Was this place and were these people for real?

He and Gretchen traveled through a maze of cobblestone streets before ending up in a large town square where people were already gathered. On a raised platform was a pair of finely dressed people. One was an older man who looked pretty kingly. David had never seen a king in person before, but he assumed this was what one would look like. He stood before the crowd and commanded everyone's attention in a regal manner. He wore long, brown fur robes that made him look like there was plenty of strength underneath. His hair was gray and black, as was the pointy thick beard on his chin. If there were still any doubt whether or not this man was king, there was a gold crown on his head.

The other person standing with him was a woman, younger, but just as well dressed. She wore a deep red dress with a white fur cape. Her blond hair was woven into a pattern that spilled down her back. This girl must have been the king's daughter because she wore a matching crown of silver.

The king was speaking, addressing the crowd that had gathered. He seemed to be in the middle of a very important speech, but that didn't stop Gretchen from interrupting.

"My Lord!" she yelled. "I have found your visitor!"

The king stopped talking and looked out to the crowd to find the small voice that was Gretchen's. She was found for him, though, when the rest of the crowd stepped back and formed a circle around her and David. The king on his platform squinted in their direction and motioned for them to come closer. The crowd parted, and they made their way to the platform and climbed up.

When David was on the platform, the king circled him, studying him up and down before speaking. Once again, David really wished he weren't in his pajamas. He thought the king was going to criticize his dress code, but he was wrong.

"We were expecting you earlier," he said.

"I'm sorry. Expecting me?" David replied.

"You are a visitor, correct?" he asked.

"Yes…"

"We have long prepared for this day but thought it would never come. We have been left alone for centuries. Now, here you are! It's settled." The way he said it almost had David convinced as well. What was settled? "We don't get visitors in Ethelrod, none until you. The one we have been waiting for."

"Waiting for? Wait—what?"

"Take him!" Men and women started to grab at him excitedly. Gretchen tried to intervene.

"Take me? What is going on here?" David managed to shout, as he was forced off the stage.

"We can now begin our contest!" the king yelled to the crowd.

Everyone cheered.

What on earth had David just stumbled into?

Chapter Five

David was shoved into a room, and the door slammed behind him. He tried to open it, even though he heard it bolt tight. No luck; it was locked.

He had had no time to register anything as he was quickly whisked away. While being pushed and shoved, David heard and saw snapshots around him that he could not make sense of: the king bending down to Gretchen, who was whispering in his ear and showing him something in her bag, the well-dressed woman on the platform talking to a man on the ground holding tightly to a sword at his belt. She said to the man, "Maybe I can talk to him. There is no need for that yet."

Something told him that the pants, boots, mail shirt, and sword on a nearby bed were laid out for him. No way was David going to have anything to do with them. In fact, he purposely stayed on the opposite side of the room. Any contest that included these items was sure to end badly.

It seemed like David was there for hours before anything happened. He heard some bolts on the door moving, and Gretchen entered. The door locked again behind her.

"You're not dressed," she said, like there was no reason in the world for him not to have changed his clothes. She had though. She wasn't as finely dressed as the others he had seen in town, but she now looked more like a girl.

"Gretchen!" David found himself yelling. "What is going on?!"

"It's an ancient tradition," she explained. "All visitors to Ethelrod are to partake in a special contest. We haven't had a visitor in centuries, so it is very exciting that you have come to us."

"What is this contest? What am I doing here?"

"The contest is a challenge. A duel. To the death. For the right to marry the princess."

"This is crazy! I don't belong here. I'm not doing it," he protested wildly.

"You don't have a choice."

"Hold on! I'm just a kid in high school. I can't fight a warrior. I can't marry a princess. I can't marry anyone! I'm too young. I don't even have a girlfriend. And fighting? I don't even think I can—"

Gretchen slapped him across the face. She had quite some power for a little girl. "Listen up, David. You don't have a choice. A refusal to partake in the contest means execution. You have to fight."

"Let me get this straight. I fall asleep and wake up here. Now, I have to fight or die, but if I fight I may die. All this because I am not supposed to be here! I don't even want to marry this princess."

"It's an ancient custom. And we are a very traditional people. We follow customs all of the time." That jogged David's memory.

"Why were you meeting the king?" David asked. "What custom were you following?"

"I found something. A treasure," Gretchen said. "We are a poor people and all found treasure must be turned in to the king for the good of the kingdom. If we do not share as a people, there is a punishment. So, I was turning in what I found in the woods when I found you."

"What was it?"

"You should worry about your upcoming battle. You are about to fight the best warrior we have. If you win, you will marry the princess. If he wins, the kingdom gets to keep its princess."

"But that means I'm dead."

"Well, yes. So let's try to not let that happen."

"I won't do it!" David yelled. "I'm just a kid. I can't fight your best warrior. And, I can't get married!"

"I'm sorry, David. This is the custom of our land, and it's our tradition. You must abide by it…or I don't know what will happen."

David was about to yell, NO, but the look on Gretchen's face told him that there was no other way.

After a huge sigh, he said, "I don't like it, but I guess I have to."

With a small smile, Gretchen said, "Okay. Good. Let's get you ready."

She helped him change into the clothes laid out for him and explained that the contest would begin at dawn. When she left, the door was once again locked, and David had no choice but to wait until morning.

David couldn't sleep. The mattress was made of straw. Or hay. David never knew the difference. Was there a difference? All David did know was that it made a crummy mattress. Any time he moved, the rustling noise brought him back out of his almost-slumber. It reminded him of his first night at Mr. Linden's when he was also unable to sleep.

That night was David's first night alone in a strange and unfamiliar place. What were his parents thinking? They sent him to live in a house that was not his, be in a room that was not his, sleep in a bed that was not his, and be under the protection of an uncle that definitely was not his. With all of this going through David's head, he was definitely not sleeping in this not-his bed. David tossed and turned but could not make himself comfortable. The pillow was hard, his legs were getting tangled in the sheets, and David was getting frustrated.

I have to get out.

David decided to go for a walk. He thought he remembered his way around the place after the tour Mr. Linden had given him when he arrived, but it was different in the dark. Everything seemed strange and unnatural in the blackness streaked with random rays of moonlight. He couldn't remember the difference between which halls had the marble floors, or that Persian carpet, or this painting of some old woman. It may not have helped that he started to change floors using main stairways and smaller staircases. As much as David didn't want to admit it, he was lost.

Should I start calling out for help?

That'd be far too embarrassing.

David turned a corner and up ahead saw light coming from under a door. If anyone were in there, they could help him find his way back. He could pretend he was trying to find the bathroom.

Wait, isn't there a bathroom right next to my room?

"I'm going to need a better excuse than that," David admitted.

If anything else, maybe he would remember which room this was, and it would help him find his bearings. David placed his hands on the brass handles and pushed open the double doors.

The light was coming from a gently roaring fire in the fireplace at a distance across the room. He made his way into the room and bumped his leg on something.

"What was that?"

It took David a while to adjust to the dancing light. He had hit a table. His eyes surveyed the room and the arrangement of tables and seating.

"I'm in the library!" Now David knew exactly how to get back to his room.

He was shown a billiards room, a ballroom, a conservatory, and all of the other rooms imaginable on the board game "Clue." At the end of the tour, Mr. Linden opened the same double set of French doors with brass handles and led David into the library. It was filled with couches, end tables, loveseats, easy chairs, wingback chairs, and tables surrounded by wooden chairs and numerous different types of lamps. Every item stood on a thick carpet that muffled their footsteps as they walked into the center of the vast room. This was the tallest room David had yet seen on his tour. "This is my favorite room," Mr. Linden said.

He motioned to David to take a look around. When he did, David noticed that the walls were not plastered in checkered wallpaper like he first thought. Instead, from floor to carved elliptical ceiling, the walls were covered with books. There were ladders, platforms, and metal spiral staircases that could take you higher and higher to reach more books than David had ever believed possible. He lost his breath at how impressive this room actually was. *But then again,* he thought, *it's only books.*

What a waste. An entire room full of pages and pages that no one had time anymore to sit down and read. David doubted Mr. Linden had even come close to reading half of one of these expansive walls full of books. Paperback, hardcover, they all were neatly lined up and ready to be read. David knew it wouldn't be him. If he were to bet, David would wager that there wasn't even one book in this room that could keep his attention.

If it never happens in school, it certainly isn't going to happen here during my time off.

Sure, he had nothing better to do this summer living in a stranger's house, but David never imagined he'd ever be desperate enough to read.

"Why is this your favorite room?" David asked.

Mr. Linden hadn't looked at him but continued to stare at the numerous shelves and smiled.

"Each book is an adventure, David, multiple adventures of every sort imaginable. Open a book and anything could happen; anything is possible. And they only end when you close the book. It's that simple." He gazed at the books as if recalling each adventure he had been able to live out because of one of those books. Then, his face grew blank, and he looked down at his new guest. "You should be careful, David," he warned. "It's easy to get lost in here."

David assumed Mr. Linden meant it was easy to get lost in the library or Mr. Linden's mansion, but he felt pretty confident he wouldn't be getting lost in a library or even stepping foot in it again, for that matter. And yet, here he was. By mistake, David had returned in the middle of the night to a room he never wanted to see again. Although David didn't really want to admit it, the room was also pretty creepy in the dark. However, at least now he had his bearings and could find his way back to his room.

David turned to leave but was stopped by a sudden noise. *Thump!* He turned back quickly and focused his eyes on the far corner.

"What was that?" David whispered.

Through tall windows on either side of the marble fireplace, faint moonlight entered the room. David could see nothing in the dim light and decided to go closer.

Was there someone else in the room? Was it just a bird that had hit one of the windows?

David kept walking.

He weaved his way around tables, chairs, couches, and lamps but found nothing. David was in the corner now, next to the window beside the fireplace. Had he just imagined it? His eyes slowly surveyed the room. Then, they found the bookshelves and his eyes traveled slowly up the levels and levels of books. Could it have come from up there?

David turned to the right and found one of the skinny spiral staircases. His hand clutched the cold metal railing, and he started to climb. He made it to the first level, and his footsteps on the metal grated platform were so surprisingly loud that David startled himself. He looked around. Nothing. But there was something. Above him, through the holes in the other grated platforms, David could make out a shape. He decided to climb even higher.

When he reached the right level, David was surprised to find there, on the middle of the platform floor, a book. It was a thick, sturdy-looking book covered in bright red leather. The golden edges of the pages reflected some of the light from the fire below. David walked over and knelt by the book but didn't touch it. Around him were many other books of different shapes and sizes, firmly and neatly tucked into their shelves. There was only one hole on the entire level where this book must belong.

"How did you get here?" David wondered.

Did someone knock it over?

That would explain the noise he heard, but there was no one else here.

Did it just jump off? Or was it even this book that I heard?

David picked up the book and brought it with him back down the dizzying stairs to a couch for further examination. He placed the book on the coffee table in front of him.

"What makes this book so special?"

It was only a book after all. The red leather was soft and the gold pages were smooth. He turned the book on the table. There was no writing on the spine where one might usually find a title or the name of an author. The covers were equally empty. He decided to open the book to find more answers, but there were none.

The pages inside the book were completely blank.

"What kind of book is this?"

He stared at the blank pages. David watched the shadows from the fire flicker across the page. He was hypnotized watching. His eyes grew sleepy. He looked over to the open doors that would lead him out into the hall and eventually to his room. They seemed so far away. David wondered why anyone would want a house so big that it was a hike just to get to your bedroom. He thought it over and then decided to sleep right where he was on the couch. The book lay open next to him, as he crossed his arms and nuzzled his head into the crook of his elbow and closed his eyes.

Mr. Linden had warned David about getting lost.

David had woken up in a forest in a completely different country.
Maybe this is all a dream.

That thought reassured David. Maybe this time, when he fell asleep on his lumpy straw or hay mattress, he would wake up and be back in Mr. Linden's library like nothing had ever happened.

That would be nice.

Chapter Six

David woke up in the middle of the night. He stretched and was happy to be back on the couch in Mr. Linden's library. He moved his body and a rustling brought him back to life. What? David felt his hay/straw bed and looked around. He was still in his locked room somewhere in Ethelrod.

This is so not fair.

Moonlight lit the room, and David could see that he wasn't alone. A hooded figure stood in the corner. David shot up and felt around for the sword. A pale hand reached out to him.

"Wait."

David was not expecting such a soft voice from such a horrifying figure. He stopped searching for the sword. The figure reached up and removed the hood. It was the beautiful blond woman from the platform!

"Princess?" he asked.

"You know me, sir?"

"It was a pretty good guess."

She introduced herself. "I am Princess Morgana."

"What can I do for you, Princess? Why are you here in my room when I'm supposed to be fighting for your hand tomorrow morning?"

"I need your help," she said. "Please help me."

"I'm the one who needs help," David corrected.

"Then maybe we can help each other."

She explained to David the loopholes in tomorrow's contest. A contestant need not actually kill the opponent but have him in a position with no other option. David liked this thought at first. Then again, he hadn't been the best at the recent wrestling unit in gym. And those were high school boys. How was he going to beat an opponent that was the best Ethelrod had to offer? At least he didn't have to kill anyone now. And there was something about the prize as well.

"I thought the winner won the right to marry the princess." David was confused.

"No, this is a mistranslation from older texts. The winner of the contest holds the destiny of the princess," she explained.

"Which means?"

"This means that you have the option of marrying me or deciding my marriage for me. This is where my favor comes in." She continued to explain that her heart belonged to another. David assumed it was the man from the town square she was talking to who had looked like he wanted to get violent. If David had a girlfriend who was going to instantly marry some new winner of a contest, he guessed he would get violent, too. She told him that he could exchange his right to marriage for a piece of treasure, which would allow her to marry her love and would allow David to leave and try to find his way back to wherever he came from.

"I don't even know how I got here!" David said.

"Well, maybe something from the treasure room can help you return, but marrying me will not help."

"Nor will losing the contest. I bet the other guy doesn't know about the death loophole." David couldn't handle it anymore. "It's all too hard. Too difficult. I can't. I won't."

"Do you only do things that are easy? Do you give up when things don't go your way?" Morgana questioned.

David wasn't sure why, but he thought about the books in school he never even started. He knew they would be a challenge, so he never even opened them. He just pretended to read them instead. What was wrong with taking shortcuts if it meant he wouldn't look like an idiot in class? He did what he knew he'd be good at and therefore never failed.

"So?" David replied.

"Just because something is tough or difficult, it doesn't mean that it isn't possible. The challenge is what makes something wonderful when you finally overcome your obstacles. The sense of success that comes from working hard over time is much better than achieving a simple task. Don't be afraid of a challenge when it can make you a better person in the end."

Princess Morgana was right. David agreed to help her and hopefully help himself get home somehow. All of this, however, depended on David surviving the contest.

The next morning, David woke up to trumpets and cheering. Gretchen told him the contest would happen in the square. He guessed the crowd was already gathered. David wondered if someone was going to come and get him soon, when the door burst open and numerous hands pulled him out into the square. A small section had been roped off.

That must be for the fight. Not too big of a space. Great.

It felt like one million hands were pushing him closer. His heart was racing, and David could feel it beating in his throat. He was tossed into the fighting section and looked around. There was no one else in the ring with him, but David did find a comforting face outside the ring.

"Gretchen!" He ran to the little girl, her hair still in braids.

"Don't die today, David. It's harder to have a life if you are dead."

"I'll try not to! I'm not a big fan of that option either. Where is this guy I'm fighting?" he asked.

"Here he comes now." Gretchen pointed to a section in the crowd that parted for the best warrior they had to send. He was a large man with huge muscles, and David probably only came up to his chest. He got to the ring and held out his hand, feeling for the rope to climb over. A short man next to him whispered instructions as the warrior fumbled over the rope.

"What's wrong with him?"

"He's blind," Gretchen answered. "But do not let that trick you. His other senses are extremely strong. He truly is the best warrior Ethelrod has to offer. And the most deadly. Watch yourself, David."

The king gave a short speech on his platform, as Princess Morgana stood next to him watching anxiously. After the speech, he rang a bell, and the crowd cheered so loudly it sounded as if a bomb were going off.

David barely had time to notice that the fight had begun when a huge blade swung by his face. That first blow almost took his ear off. He could still hear the ringing left behind by his opponent's sword cutting the air so near his face. It wasn't necessarily the best face in the world, but it was his, so David tried to keep it, and himself, as far away from danger as possible. This, of course, was easier said than done when staring down a gargantuan warrior whose only purpose was to hack you into a million tiny pieces.

How did he get to this point? Everything had escalated so quickly!

David could have created a list of people to blame, but he was too busy ducking another swing of the sword and somersaulting away from his opponent. Now backed into a corner, the mammoth of a man ran toward him swinging his hungry sword. David froze. He couldn't even think. The only thing David knew to be true as he looked near-death in the face was that a week ago he never would have predicted this would be in store for him for his summer vacation.

His opponent swung his sword at David again. It would have

chopped him in half if he hadn't moved to the right just in time. As he ran to the other side of the ring, the fighter's head followed him and so did his blade. David stood still for a moment, and the warrior seemed to lose him in the cheering of the crowd. This might work. Just don't move, nothing will happen, and maybe they will just end the contest.

The warrior did not cooperate with that plan. He screamed and started swinging his sword all over in an attempt to hit David, or at least make him reveal himself.

"You can't hide forever," he yelled in his deep voice.

David reached for his sword and pulled it out of its sheath. Of course, the warrior heard this, slashed his sword through the air, and knocked David's sword out of his hand. The crowd grew silent. David was worried.

"I can hear your breathing, boy. You scared?"

The warrior lunged his sword straight at David, but he ducked and somersaulted just in time toward his sword, skidding across a noisy pile of rubble.

"Running away are you?" the fighter called out in David's direction.

Gretchen was right; this guy was good.

David started to stand up, and the pebbles at his feet made even more noise. The warrior started rushing at him. Without even thinking, he knew what to do. David picked up a pebble and tossed it across the ring so that it clattered on the cobblestones on the opposite side. The warrior skidded to a halt. He turned in the other direction, away from David. David kept at it. He threw handfuls of rocks in that direction making as much noise as he could. The warrior kept striking the air and ground trying to find what he thought was David. If David were going to win this, he had to do it quickly. He threw the last of the pebbles at his feet and ran toward the warrior. Hearing noises from both sides, the warrior struggled to make a decision. This delay was all David needed to slash the fighter's leg and bring him crashing to the ground, dropping his sword. With his foot,

David held down the warrior's chest and put the tip of his sword to the man's throat.

"Don't move if you want to live," David told him.

He looked up eagerly at the platform. The king was confused, but Princess Morgana was whispering what David hoped were the loopholes of this ancient contest.

The king stood up and announced, "We have our champion!"

The applause was thundering. The same hands that had pushed him into the ring that morning pulled David up onto the platform with the king and his daughter.

"And here is your future bride," the king said, as he shoved David toward Princess Morgana.

"Actually, your highness," David started, "I would like an exchange."

"Exchange?" the king roared. "My daughter is not good enough for a lowly visitor?"

"Father," Princess Morgana interrupted. "Let him speak. He has won that right today."

David continued. "Your highness, I choose to allow the princess to marry whom she will and command that they be wed immediately. And because I have done this, I will accept a gift from your treasury."

The king had no words but seemed to agree with the decision this time without any side conversations with his daughter.

"Very well."

On the way through the crowd to the treasury, Gretchen found David and leaped onto his back in congratulations. "You did it!" she screamed.

"I did! And now I need your help once more. I'm on my way to find something in the treasury that will hopefully help get me home." Gretchen nodded and agreed to help him search.

The guard left them alone in the treasury and told David he was allowed to pick only one item, but it could be any item he chose. Gretchen instantly shot off, and David lost her running through the mountains of gold objects. It was hard to believe what Gretchen said about this being a poor kingdom when this room was filled with so much stuff.

David sifted through the items and could not find any maps. There were no compasses, nothing to help him find out where he was or how to get back to where he came from. David was getting frustrated when he heard a familiar giggle behind him. He turned to see Gretchen, her hands behind her back.

"David," she said. "I think this might help."

From behind her, she revealed a brightly shining golden object that was moving quite quickly. Sheets of gold were constantly flipping around. What was this thing? David looked closer. It was a book! The golden sheets were pages. The book lay flat in Gretchen's hands and the pages appeared to be constantly turning as fast as possible, while never reaching the end of the book. David took it gently in his hands, but the object felt familiar. He looked even more closely. This book had a bright red leather cover and golden pages. Just like the book from Mr. Linden's library!

David felt the bump on his head. Everything was starting to come back now. That first night in the library, he lay down on the couch, crossed his arms, and nuzzled his head into the crook of his elbow and closed his eyes. Yet David did not fall asleep. There was too much light coming from the direction of the fireplace. David could almost see it through his eyelids. David opened his eyes, but it was not the fire that they fell upon. It was the book in front of him on the coffee table.

Whether it was from the fire or not, the gold lining of the book's pages began to glow softly. Slowly, little hairs seemed to be growing out from the spine in between the pages. Was the firelight playing tricks on his eyes? Was this a symptom of not getting enough sleep? Then, David noticed they weren't hairs. They were vines that sprouted leaves and gently crawled their way out of the book. They twisted their way across the table and down the legs toward the floor that was no longer covered in a thick carpet but grass and dirt. Around David, couches turned to boulders and from the legs of lamps sprung trees growing high beyond the curved ceiling that was no longer present. Instead, they rose up into a dark, starry night. A forest appeared as the library slipped away.

David didn't know what to do. How was one supposed to react when a room was transforming and being taken over by nature? He watched in awe as more trees were spontaneously shooting out of the ground, higher and higher. He jumped back as one came directly in front of him, but he went too far. Behind him, another tree sprang up and a branch bashed David in the back of the head. He felt dizzy and collapsed onto the nearby couch.

He was groggy, but he could feel one final tree rise. It came out of the ground right underneath David's couch, taking it up into the air with David still in it. David felt the rush of wind as he was transported higher and higher into the branches of the massive tree. David tried to stay strong, but his head hurt and he couldn't keep his eyes open anymore.

David remembered now. That book. That same book that magically transported him from Mr. Linden's library and into the kingdom of Ethelrod was now again in his hands, thanks to the help of a little girl.

"This is my book!" David screamed in excitement. "But how did you—"

"I told you," Gretchen explained. "All treasure must be turned in directly to the king or else. I didn't know what to do. I didn't even know you then or that it actually was yours. It was just there on the table. I didn't even notice anyone else was around until you woke up and fell out of that tree. I'm sorry, David. I didn't think it would be that important. It is only a book after all."

"Open a book and anything could happen," David repeated. He remembered Mr. Linden saying something about that. "Anything is possible. And it only ends when you close the book."

"Is that it? Is that how you will get home?" Gretchen asked.

"It's that simple."

David tried pushing the covers of the book together, but it was harder than he thought. It was like pushing two repelling magnets together against their will. The pages kept turning and as the covers got closer and closer together, the golden light from the pages became brighter. As David was about to close the book, the light became so focused and so bright that he had to clamp his eyes shut so they wouldn't burn right out of their sockets.

When David opened his eyes again, there was only daylight. He could feel his arm against his face. He sat up to find himself in a chair at a table. Where was he now? David quickly looked around. The walls of the room seemed familiarly filled with books. Two tall windows let in the morning light, as the remaining smoke smoldered on a dying fire in the marble fireplace between them. David was in Mr. Linden's library. He was back!

Did he ever leave? David found the red book he had discovered the night before on the table in front of him. The book was closed. Had he simply dreamt it all? David looked around even more for a signal, some type of sign; instead he found a face.

Sitting in a wingback chair nearby was Mr. Linden, smiling at him. "I told you it was easy to get lost in here."

"But I never even left," David objected. "I was here the whole time. I'm still in my pajamas!"

"If you say so, then."

David got up to leave but knocked something over onto the floor. It clattered and clanged as it fell, and David went to see what it was. There on the carpet was a sword. Not just any sword but the sword he had just been fighting with only moments ago. It did happen. It had to have happened.

A smile of joyous realization spread out over his face. David quickly looked up at Mr. Linden and his matching smile and said, "This is my favorite room!"

Chapter Seven

David woke up to a familiar throbbing pain in his neck. The red leather, golden-paged book was open exactly where he left it. He felt disappointment and then a sharp ache as he raised his head off the couch. It was not the most comfortable sleeping choice considering the vast number of rooms in Mr. Linden's house.

"Did you sleep in the library again?"

Mr. Linden stood in the open doorway.

David looked around the tall, expansive room that reminded him of something like a cathedral. It could have been the large floor-to-ceiling windows on either side of the massive marble fireplace, or it might have been the reverence he felt when looking around at the platforms and staircases that led to the numbers of books covering the walls and enclosing the room's chairs, couches, tables, and lamps.

He looked back at Mr. Linden. "I thought it would work this time." David looked back at the book. "I could feel it."

He wanted to feel the way he did on his adventure to Ethelrod, sword fighting and near-death experiences included. David longed for it as he looked at the sword he had brought back with him that now hung over the library's fireplace. It was tangible proof that Ethelrod wasn't just a dream.

Since that night, David had tried to relive those circumstances in order to find himself on another adventure in some other world. He would go back to the same couch, in front of a new coffee table since he had broken the last one. David would fall asleep with the open book in his arms. But every morning, he woke up back in Mr. Linden's library, still his regular self.

Yet, not quite his regular self exactly. Before coming to Mr. Linden's this summer, David would never have caught himself volunteering to spend time in a library of all places. He would spend hours outside throwing his lacrosse ball against the side of the house practicing. It would hit the wall, and then David would catch it again. He would repeat the process with his other hand. Throw, hit, catch, switch. Throw, hit, catch, switch.

Now, something had changed within him. Maybe it was just all of his time spent with so many books, but David actually was starting to read on his own.

This did not happen overnight, of course. On David's second day of just staring at Mr. Linden's open book, he felt the urge to explore the numerous platforms of shelves that surrounded him. A title about sword fighting caught his eye, but as he started to read he got bored and put the book back. Unlike he had previously, however, this time David didn't give up. He kept looking for another book. He picked up a Shakespeare title he remembered hearing about because it had a bloodthirsty king in it, but there were too many words he didn't recognize so he got rid of it. At last, he found a collection of King Arthur legends and was hooked. Maybe it was because he finally had some true background knowledge about kings, queens, and knights, but he was really getting into it.

One night at dinner, David even shared his reading progress with Mr. Linden.

"It's just fine to abandon books that are too hard or don't interest you," Mr. Linden admitted. "The important things that good readers need are time, ability, and interest."

"I never thought of that," David said. "I guess it's true. I'm finally reading things I like and choosing for myself. Reading doesn't seem that bad anymore."

When he finally finished the King Arthur legends, he remembered something Princess Morgana had once told him: the sense of success that comes when working hard over time is much better than achieving a simple task. He understood this a little better now. He struggled with the reading but finished it. It was a great sense of accomplishment. It was much better than just getting summaries online. He continued to read more books.

However, David had these opportunities only because the real book he was interested in wasn't cooperating. All the books in Mr. Linden's library weren't enough to distract David from his real goal of making the red leather book work its magic once more. He kept repeating the same routine as the first night but never got lucky.

"It will work when it's ready," Mr. Linden told David.

"But you've had tons of adventures! It's not fair," David complained.

"David." Mr. Linden walked over to the table and sat down with him. "I need to tell you something."

"Okay?"

"The book hasn't opened any adventures for me in years. I was devastated. When I found out it worked for you on your first night, I was a little jealous of what you got to experience. I thought the book had run out of juice or something."

"You think I won't be able to use it again?" David couldn't believe what he was hearing.

"I think that when you came here that night, you had something the book needed in order to work. You were the one chosen to help change Ethelrod. I think that when you have whatever it needs again, you will both be ready."

"I just have to wait? Is that what you're saying? Even though it could be years?"

"Sorry, David, but that's what I'm saying," Mr. Linden replied, as he left the room.

The metal spiral staircase creaked as David walked up to the second platform in the back left corner by the tall window. He found the empty spot where the book had seemingly jumped off the shelf that first night. David put the book back into its place and half hoped it would jump out again. It didn't. David slept in his bed that night.

Chapter Eight

Next week, David did have a new experience. It was something odd in the fact that he never realized that this had never happened before. For the first time since he had come to live with Mr. Linden, the doorbell rang.

David raced through the hallways, as whoever was here rang again. He came to the foyer and slid to a stop in front of the entrance. He opened the door to find a girl about his age, reaching for the ringer for a third time. Their eyes locked. For a moment, David thought she was pretty until her face transitioned to confusion and she spat out, "Who are you?"

David was caught off guard. "Me? Uh, I—I'm David. I live here."

Unimpressed, the girl walked right past David into the house with her duffle bag. She dumped it on the floor and turned to look back at him. "I'm looking for someone else who lives here."

"Hannah?" a soft voice asked in the distance.

"Hi, Dad."

David was trying to wrap his head around all of the facts that he didn't know about the man with whom he had been living. Mr. Linden was not married, but he had a daughter show up from out of

44

nowhere. David tried to understand the weaving of stories Hannah told about moving out and trying to support herself on her own.

Wasn't she a bit young? David thought. *How was she allowed to do this?*

He heard her talk about being evicted for what he guessed was some type of fraud and somehow she ended up here.

"But don't think I'm staying for very long," Hannah added.

"Okay," Mr. Linden responded calmly.

"I just need a place to get back on my feet and then I'm gone again."

"Okay," Mr. Linden repeated.

David got the sense that Mr. Linden's relationship with his daughter was not strong enough for him to have any authority as to whether or not she was allowed to come and go whenever she wanted. To David, Mr. Linden just seemed happy that she was here.

After the newly reunited father and daughter covered all the basics, the topic switched to David.

"And who's this?" Hannah asked, looking David up and down.

"Hannah, this is David. He will be living with us this summer," Mr. Linden answered.

"Why is he living here?"

Good question, David thought. He wished he knew the answer.

Mr. Linden answered again. "David's parents are good friends of mine. He's been staying here while his parents are out of town."

"Friends? You don't have any friends, at least none that I've met or heard of. You never go out, let alone leave your library—"

"Not now, Hannah," Mr. Linden interrupted.

"How do your parents know my dad? Why did they send you here?" Hannah asked David.

David shrugged. "No one else was available, I guess."

Hannah smiled. She looked as she did when David found her on the porch. She liked his answer. "All right then."

She picked up her bag and started to walk away. She stopped and turned back. "What's your name again?" Hannah asked.

"David."

"Nice to meet you, David."

"Dinner's at seven, Hannah. It would be great if you could join us," Mr. Linden said.

Hannah rolled her eyes, and then was gone.

Mr. Linden put a hand on David's shoulder, stopping him from following.

"David," Mr. Linden confessed, "my daughter knows nothing about the red book. I would appreciate it if you didn't mention it to her."

"What? She has no idea what it is or what it can do?"

"I haven't gotten it to work since before she was born," Mr. Linden explained. "And yet, it's still one of the reasons she ran away."

"Ran away? How long has she—"

"One year. I haven't seen my daughter in one year. Sure, she sent me postcards to let me know she was alive and well, but it was clear she wanted to be anywhere but here. Away from me. I tried to send a private investigator after her once, but her postcards were from all over the country. She didn't want to be found. Now that she's home, I'd like to see that she stays."

"And the book?" David asked.

"I don't want to talk about it. I don't want her to even hear about it. If she catches wind of it, she might leave again. I can't go through that a second time." Mr. Linden stared into David's eyes. "Please, David."

"Okay," David promised. "The red book will be our secret."

Hannah may have been gone from her father's house for some time, but David noticed she was still able to tell when something was changed or added. She picked out the new chairs in the dining hall, the new drapes in the kitchen, and something a little more interesting in the library.

"What's that sword?" Hannah asked, looking back at her dad.

"It's David's, actually. He brought it back from one of his visits."

David liked his use of the word "visit." He had never thought about it before, about how he would sound to an outsider if he told the true story of where that sword had come from. They would lock him up for sure and throw away the key. He would have to be content with wearing a straitjacket and living in a room with padded walls. No, David would make sure that the sword's true story didn't get out.

"It's yours?" Hannah asked.

David nodded.

"How did you get it?"

"David won it in a contest," Mr. Linden replied quickly.

"Yeah, a contest!" David decided that it wasn't too far from the truth to be considered an actual lie. He was glad that Mr. Linden was so quick on his feet, so David let Mr. Linden do all of the talking. Although, his skills should not be that much of a surprise; surely Mr. Linden had had more experience explaining his "visits" to outsiders. David realized this secret might be harder to keep than anticipated.

Chapter Nine

It was nice to finally have someone his own age around. David could have always gone to town, but he didn't know anyone, and it was too long a distance to trek in the hopes of making any friends. He enjoyed having Hannah around. He especially loved her stories.

"And you really walked all the way to the top?" David asked.

"The view through the eyes of the Statue of Liberty is amazing. You would really like it."

David noticed she was nicer when it was just the two of them. She had more energy, a positive one that flowed out as she talked. He absorbed as much as he could.

"But the view doesn't compare to the Grand Canyon."

"You liked it, huh?"

"It's magnificent! But I'll be honest; it does get old after a while of just looking at it."

"Did you ride down to the bottom on a donkey?" David thought he saw somewhere you could do that.

"That costs money. I definitely wasn't going to waste it sitting on a smelly animal. No, thank you. When you're on your own, you need to be responsible. You are the only one looking out for you."

"Strangely, I get that," said David. "I've grown used to my parents leaving me on my own. At least this time, they dropped me on the doorstep of a stranger. In class, even though I'm smart, capable, and friendly, no one ever really asks much of me. It's the same at home."

Except, wasn't I just asked to help a princess by winning a tournament? And I had to fight their best warrior for that one.

"We have a lot in common. We both pretty much look out for ourselves."

David added, "Now we can look out for each other."

David taught Hannah how to throw and catch a lacrosse ball. She was a quick learner. That impressed him. He hoped he impressed her, too, with his skill.

During a late night ice cream binge session in the kitchen, Hannah told another story about sneaking into a concert in San Francisco. After all of their time shared, David felt comfortable enough to ask Hannah something. "But didn't you ever just want to come home?"

Hannah paused as she finished her spoonful of mint chocolate chip.

"I'm sure I didn't miss anything," she replied. "And it doesn't seem like my dad missed me very much either. If he even noticed."

"But he did," David replied. "He even sent an investigator after you."

Hannah put down her spoon and stared at David. He studied her face. *Did I just tell her something she didn't know?* Hannah's look was clear. *Did she really believe her father didn't care about her?*

Hannah picked up her spoon again. "Well, whoever he hired wasn't very good then, was he?" David heard the changed tone in her voice. It was the tone she used when Mr. Linden was in the room. "My dad could have tried harder."

How could someone actually think their parents didn't like them? David stopped. *Oh yeah, hadn't I been thinking the same thing about the parents who ditched me here? But surely there's more to my parents' story. And I bet there's more to Hannah and Mr. Linden's story, as well.*

The mood had shifted. David didn't like it. He went back to what they were good at. He gave her the usual command. "Tell me a story."

Hannah pondered for a moment. "Did I tell you about how I got kicked out of an apartment and ended up back here? I don't think I have."

"You haven't."

"Well, it's a good one, even if I'm not at my finest."

"I'm all ears," David encouraged her.

"Okay," Hannah started. "So, being a teen runaway isn't as fabulous as it was in my head. While some might say I was doing it for Daddy's attention, and they might have something there, I also just wanted to get out of this house finally and see some things. What I didn't factor into the equation was how expensive everything is! I ran out of money quickly, lived on the mercy of others, hid out, worked odd jobs, and even borrowed when necessary. All I knew was that I wasn't going home.

"Tired of second-rate living, I got a bright idea. I would get an apartment and live with my aunt. I don't really have an aunt, but I made my landlord think I did so he didn't know he was renting an apartment to a teenager. It worked until I ran out of money again. I kept telling the landlord my aunt was out and she would pay him when she got back. In the meantime, I needed a second plan to get this guy to lower the rate so I could afford rent. It was genius! I would convince the other tenants the building was haunted."

David laughed so loud he thought he might wake up Mr. Linden on the other side of the mansion. "You're joking," he said. "This can't be true."

"It is!" she said. "It's amazing what you can do with some old chains, a bit of dry ice, and the power of suggestion."

"Did it work?" David asked.

"Not really," Hannah answered. "The landlord caught me making ghost noises. He was so furious that he stormed me back to my apartment and demanded to talk to my aunt."

"What happened?"

"Well, he realized there wasn't even a second tenant. I guess he wasn't as dumb as I thought. He was so furious that he threw me out and threatened to call the cops."

"What did you do next?"

"Coming back here was my last choice, but I didn't have any other options. Maybe I was getting tired of the whole thing…so here I am!"

"And here you are," David repeated. "And think of it, if you never decided to come home, we never would have met and become friends. And who would you have to tell your stories to?"

"Your turn," she said. "Tell me a story."

He wanted to compete with her stories, but the best he had to tell he promised himself he wouldn't. His life experiences before coming to Mr. Linden's didn't really compare to hers, but he did his best.

There was one thing they could talk about though: books. David had never thought about using books as a way of building relationships between people, but it seemed to work. In the library, Hannah would recommend titles that David had never even heard of but ended up loving. Why had he never been assigned books like these in school? Maybe he would have enjoyed reading earlier.

Even better than reading Hannah's recommendations was getting to talk with her about them. He loved hearing her point of view on plots and characters, even if he disagreed, and they ended up in friendly battles. Talking about these titles allowed David to grow closer to Hannah in a way he never thought books could do in class. However, he couldn't get too close, because David still had a big secret of his own to hide.

He wanted to share with her. He wanted her to listen to one of his life stories with as much emotion as she told hers, but he couldn't yet. Not this story. This story would have her running out the door as fast as she could, thinking he was out of his mind. He definitely didn't want to ruin whatever this was. *What was this, anyway?*

Chapter Ten

One night after a long day, David found himself unable to sleep. This time it wasn't the uncomfortable couch keeping him awake. Tonight, he just wasn't tired. He tried flipping through the pages of a magazine he kept on his nightstand, but it was no use. He knew what he really wanted to do. David got out of bed and made the long walk to the library.

He felt the excitement tingling as he got closer and closer. It was different this time. This time the book would work. He would find a way to make it work. He had to.

David opened the French doors to the library and basked in the glory of it all. The fireplace was lit, giving the room a soft glow. It was still dim, but David was able to maneuver around tables and chairs without a problem. He had already figured out the best route to the back corner and had made the journey so many times he could do it with or without light. David was just past the middle of the room when something startled him.

"David?" the voice said.

He quickly turned around and tried to focus on the area around him. There was a lump on a nearby couch, and he strained his eyes to make out an image.

"Hannah? Is that you? What are you doing?" he asked.

"My dad and I got into another fight," she admitted. "He said I didn't think about my choices and their consequences enough, that I make decisions too quickly before thinking what could happen eventually down the road. That's funny coming from him."

Hannah was curled up on a couch with a book under her arm. "I couldn't sleep so I was just, just trying to…I don't know." David sat down beside her, and she continued. "When I was a little girl, my dad loved this room. I remember he would come in here, pick out a book, and I wouldn't see him all day. I thought maybe I would try to figure out what was so great about it, so great that he would rather be in here than spend time with me. Part of the reason I ran away the first time was to see if he'd even notice."

David didn't know what to say. She wasn't looking directly at him, but she kept talking.

"I saw him with this book a number of times. I think it was his favorite." She pulled out the book from under her arm. It was *the* book. "I picked it out to see why it was so important, but you know what's funny? It's blank. All of it. There's nothing written on any of these pages." Hannah leaned her head on the arm of the couch and sighed. "Tell me a story."

David had already used his good ones up. He really didn't have anything left she hadn't already heard before.

He looked at the fire. It danced with its red, yellow, and blue flames. He drew his eyes up to the sword and then back to the book now pressed to Hannah's chest. He was not sure why he did it. Maybe it was the way the light of the fire hit her face or something.

"Want to hear how I got that sword?" he asked.

"Sure!"

"It actually has a lot to do with that book."

Hannah sat up and listened as he told her the fantastic story of the book and his visit to Ethelrod, the duel, and how his friend Gretchen helped him use the book to return back here. Hannah was excited and scared at all the right places, which made David go into greater detail and be even more dramatic in the story's telling.

"And that," David finished, "explains how hundreds of adventures can be had just by opening a book."

Hannah looked back at the book in her hands. She placed it on the coffee table and went to the window. "It's morning," she announced. "Thank you for trying to convince me that this is more than just a book. But it's just reading. They're just books. Nothing all that special, even if my dad thinks so." She placed her hand on David's shoulder. "Thank you." She leaned over and kissed him on the cheek before walking away. "And that was quite a story. You have a real imagination."

"Hannah," David called.

"Yeah?"

"That was a real story."

She giggled. "Okay, David. Whatever you say."

"Hannah, I'm serious!" He had told her his secret, and she didn't believe it.

The weeks and weeks of pain, frustration, and disappointment from trying to get that magic book to come alive again had finally come bubbling to the surface. He picked up the book and started waving it around.

"David?"

"I have waited for so long. I was patient. I hoped that something would happen. It'll probably never work again, and I'm stuck here. Stuck here for good." A single tear rolled down his cheek and splashed onto the cover before David gave the book a final slam back on the coffee table. "I'm done." David stormed off.

"David, wait," Hannah called. "Come back."

David was almost to the door when a huge burst of wind slammed the doors shut in front of him. David turned to check the windows. They weren't open, but something else was. He started running back to the coffee table. "Look! The book!"

Hannah joined him. "What about–oh, my gosh! It's glowing!" she screamed. "How is that—Why is it—" She looked in shock at David. "What's happening?"

"I think it's working. I don't really know because I was knocked unconscious last time, but this could be it."

He kept looking from her to the book, anxious not to miss anything, whatever it was that was happening. He watched and waited for more vines to appear like last time. He eagerly looked around the room to check if trees were sprouting from the floor again. Nothing yet.

"Look!" Hannah pointed to the center of the book. Small water drops were clearly visible on the book's pages. Nothing was leaking from the ceiling. The drops got bigger. Small drips started appearing between the pages and falling onto the table. The drips slowly became more frequent, and then the book quickly started squirting out more water.

"Stand back," David suggested. They both stood staring down at the book as it started gushing more and more water onto the floor and around their feet.

"David?" Hannah rocked back and forth on her feet.

"Wait."

Water continued to pour out of the book at a faster pace.

Suddenly, a geyser burst out between the pages at the spine and almost reached the library ceiling.

"Run!" David screamed, as the water crashed around them, soaking them both.

They had only made it to the next table by the time the water in the library was up to their knees. The water kept falling from above and rising up their legs. It was now at their waists, as some tables and chairs started floating on the surface.

"What do we do?" Hannah yelled over the roar of the water.

"Over here!" David pointed to one of the library staircases, and they waded toward it. Once they reached it, they pulled themselves over the railing and started making their ascent. The water rose quickly, following closely behind them as they climbed upward. They made it to the top platform and could go no further.

"Now what?" Hannah yelled.

The water stopped rising and suddenly went calm. It was just below their feet.

"What the heck is this?!" Hannah was screaming. "Is this normal for you?!"

"I'm pretty sure this isn't what happened last time," David replied.

"Last time? You mean that story was true?!"

They looked out over the vast lake that had just relocated to Mr. Linden's library. The surface was littered with books, tables, and chairs, some floating softly before sinking down. All seemed quiet. Then, from the middle of the room, a loud rumble sounded. The rumble turned into a gurgle as the water started quickly moving around the room. Instantly, there was a giant whirlpool sucking all of the water and everything in it back toward its center. The pieces of furniture violently crashed into one another, filling the water with more debris before sucking the pieces to the center and below. The sounds were intense.

"No, I'm definitely sure it wasn't like this!" David yelled.

The water spun around the room at lightning speed. It carried a table that crashed into one of the staircases and shook the platform where David and Hannah stood.

"Hold onto something," David told Hannah, but soon enough another piece of library furniture crashed into the platform and sent both of them over the railing and into the water.

David broke the surface and coughed, gulping for air. He couldn't control the direction his body moved but swung his arms around searching for Hannah. His right hand found her shirt. She was also coughing for air, but she grabbed onto his arm. David's vision was blurred as Hannah and he were thrust around the room. He could see, though, that they were coming closer to the vortex. Hannah was pulled underwater, and David was forced under with her. The spinning became faster, the pressure more intense. David felt his lungs ache and then fill with water. He held onto Hannah as the pressure became too much to bear. Everything was becoming darker. He fought, but blackness took him. Then there was nothing.

avid was too weak to open his eyes. Suddenly, he was hit with a blast of water. David could almost make out the sound. He focused again on crashing water. He rocked his head back and forth and wiggled his fingers. Wet sand.

Am I on a beach?

Another surge of cold salt water splashed his face. Yes, he was on a beach.

It startled him, and David opened his eyes. His face against the shore, he saw the long expanse of white sand and blue water. He also saw two legs running toward him before he closed his eyes again. He felt his body being turned over. He forced his eyes open again to see a blurry face that looked female. He tried to focus, but David had no strength and found the darkness closing in on him again. Did this person just say his name?

The next time David opened his eyes, he was noticeably stronger. He felt warmer. He was covered in something soft. A blanket. There was a pillow under his head. He started to stir as he woke up and heard someone walking toward him. He opened his eyes to the same blurry face he had seen on the beach. He blinked a few more times to get a clearer image. She was attractive, with a soft face and long brown hair that came down over her shoulders. She smiled at him as if she knew him.

Do I know her?

David thought hard as he studied the face. He must have seemed a bit confused because she started to giggle.

"Gretchen?"

"Hello, David," she answered in a kind voice.

As Gretchen sat down on the bed with him, David looked her over. She was no longer the young child that he had met in the woods on his first day in Ethelrod.

He was back in Ethelrod and once again hers was the first face he saw. It was somewhat comforting.

"You grew up," David said in surprise.

"Time must move faster here because you don't seem to have changed at all," she replied. "You look exactly as you did on the day you disappeared right before my eyes. I never thought I'd see you again. I had no idea where you went."

"Yeah, sorry about leaving like that."

"People thought I was insane when I returned from the treasury without you, saying you vanished into thin air. Even Ethelrod has not been the same since you left."

"I only saw you about two-and-a-half months ago. How long have I been gone?"

"It's been almost ten years since you left."

"Ten years?!"

"So you can understand my surprise to find you and your friend on the beach this morning."

"My friend? Hannah!" David sat up straight in bed. "Where is she? Is she all right?"

"She seems fine, but she is in a little bit of shock." Gretchen pointed to a body crouched in the corner of the small, plain, and modest room. David flung off the blanket and went over to her. He could hear her softly mumbling. He put his hand on her shoulder.

"Hannah? Hannah, it's me, David."

She looked up at him with a scared look. Suddenly, she started searching quickly around the room. The next words out of her mouth were strung together with such speed it was hard to understand. "We shouldn't be here. How did we get here? I don't belong here. What am I doing here?"

David put both of his hands on her shoulders and got closer to her face. "Hannah? Hannah!" She stopped as their eyes met.

"David?"

"It's me. I'm here. You're safe," he assured her.

Hannah wrapped her arms around him so fast, he was caught off guard and fell over. It took a while to get back upright and finish calming Hannah down.

"Hannah, there is someone I would like you to meet." He walked Hannah over and introduced her to Gretchen.

"Gretchen." Hannah thought a while. "You mean the girl from last night's story? No, that's impossible. That—that would mean we are in—that we are actually in…"

"Ethelrod," Gretchen finished.

"David," Hannah asked, "does that mean the book? The book actually brought us here, like you said?"

"Yep!" This seemed like an inadequate response, but it was all that David had at the moment.

"Wait a minute. Gretchen. I thought you said she was a little girl. She looks the same age as us!"

"I think time works differently here," David explained. "Apparently, it's been ten years."

"This is too weird."

"David," Gretchen interrupted. "My age isn't the only thing that has changed while you were gone."

"I bet," he replied. "I must have been brought back for a specific reason. What do you guys need me to do this time? Rescue another princess? Fight a giant? Something like that?"

"What are you talking about?" Hannah interjected. "We're going home. Now!"

"We can't," David tried to reason. "I know I have a purpose for being back. I can feel it. Something is wrong, possibly because of what happened on my first trip or we wouldn't have come to Ethelrod. My choices and actions must have set something into motion, so it's our responsibility to do whatever we can to help."

"No, not 'our,'" Hannah disagreed. "Those were *your* choices, *your* consequences. I want nothing to do with them. I don't want to help anyone. I want to go home where we belong."

David thought for a moment. She wasn't exactly wrong. "The book probably won't let us go home until we do what we came to do."

"The book won't *let* us," Hannah said in disbelief. "I don't want this. I'm going to stay here where I don't have to make any choices."

"Even choosing not to act is still a choice with possible consequences," David pointed out.

David watched Hannah. He knew that look. *She knows I'm right, but there's no way she'll admit it was me who convinced her.*

It was Gretchen who broke the silence. "I'm not sure why you have been brought back, but it is clear that David is most likely the only one who can help us out." David felt a puff of pride build up in his chest. Gretchen walked over to the wardrobe and continued. "But, David, for right now, I need you to wear this."

"A dress!" David exclaimed.

"Now I'm totally in for this adventure," Hannah said, laughing. "Let's do this."

Chapter Twelve

"When you first came, you allowed Princess Morgana to marry any man she chose. Soon after you vanished, Morgana's father died, making her Queen Morgana. She did not remain married for long as her chosen husband died in what was declared a jousting accident, even though no one has fully disproven the rumor of foul play. She continued to rule with her chief advisor, Lord Valstayne, by her side for what was predicted to be an era of progress and peace."

"That doesn't sound so bad," David said.

"This, however, was not the case. After her husband's death, because of Queen Morgana's right to choose her own husband, chaos ensued. High-ranking men in Ethelrod began to fight over who should become the next king. If one man started to have noticeable favor with Morgana, he was soon killed, for everyone else assumed that they would be the next reasonable choice and got rid of the competition."

"Men," Hannah scoffed.

"Hey!" David protested. "That's not fair."

"Okay, all right," Hannah consented.

Gretchen went on. "Warring lords formed alliances to eliminate their rivals before turning on their friends. Even more attractive men from the lower classes, who some thought might catch the queen's eye, were either imprisoned or executed for some reason or another."

"It's not a safe time to be a male in Ethelrod while Morgana remains single," Hannah commented.

"This is why," Gretchen explained, "we have to hide you, David. If people learn that the same champion who helped Morgana years ago has returned, then you will be in danger."

"Why?" David asked.

"Because you'd be a logical choice for Morgana to pick as a husband," Hannah answered. "Even if you are still the same teenager as before."

"Exactly," Gretchen agreed.

David didn't like the idea, but if it meant fewer people would want him dead, he was willing to put on the dress and have more fabric wrapped around his head to hide his face and the beginnings of facial hair. Hannah was also given a dress of her own, so she would fit in better with the crowd.

"Isn't this wonderful?" Hannah swooned. "Isn't it exciting to be in a time of kings and queens and lords?"

"Sure, I guess," he said. "We aren't going to find out what brought us here if we stay cooped up inside. I guess we ought to go look around."

"Do you think if you complete whatever we need to do, we can go home?" Hannah asked.

"Of course, to get home all we have to do is…? Wait, Gretchen, where is the book?!" David became frantic. "We need the book to get home!"

"David," Gretchen said in her calming voice, "I have the book. It is safe." She walked back over to the wardrobe and opened it up for all to see. There on the shelf was the book from Mr. Linden's library.

"It's beautiful," Hannah exclaimed.

The book lay open on a shelf in the wardrobe. Its red cover was slightly visible but overshadowed by the pages, which were constantly flipping as if moved by the wind. But there was no wind. They kept moving and yet they never got closer to the end, as if an infinite amount of paper was being supplied. To top that, the gilded pages were glowing with a golden light. David and Hannah just stared at it.

They were interrupted as Gretchen closed the wardrobe door. "We should go."

Gretchen's family lived in a rural fishing town on the western shores of Ethelrod. A long walk, or a shorter ride, through the woods would lead you to where Morgana's castle was located, as well as the town square where David had fought years ago. He wondered if it still looked the same. It had many shops and houses, all connected by neat cobblestone streets. It was much grander than Gretchen's fishing town, where everything seemed smaller and slightly dirtier, but the residents here were just as happy. Many people in the marketplace greeted Gretchen as she walked by.

"This place is pretty cool," David commented.

"How are we supposed to know what to do?" Hannah asked. "You know, before we are able to close the book and go home?"

"I'm not sure," David answered. "Maybe it will just come to us."

As he said this, he tripped over the hem of his skirt and knocked into a table. A few apples tumbled to the ground. David apologized, but the vendor didn't seem to mind. Gretchen and Hannah didn't notice and kept walking. David reached down to pick up the fruit and was met by another overlapping rough hand. He looked up at the face of an older, middle-aged man, with a few wrinkles on his tan face around his eyes and a smile poking through a dark, thick goatee.

Hold on. Did this man just wink at me?

David stood up fast and quickly checked his face to make sure it was covered well enough.

"Oh, excuse me, Miss," the man said, holding his hand out apologetically. "I did not mean to frighten you."

David looked around trying to find Gretchen and Hannah. He

noticed this man studying his face, so he tried looking away.

"Excuse me," he continued, "I take pride in knowing everyone here, but you are less familiar. Do I know you?"

David shook his head.

"What is your name?" he asked. David was unsure why, but this man seemed to be moving closer. *Doesn't he know about personal space?*

David decided he couldn't pantomime forever. "Da—" he started, but his voice was too low. He coughed and tried again at a higher pitch, "Da—Daphne."

"Well, Daphne," he moved closer again, almost touching him. David was starting to get very uncomfortable. "How is it I don't know a girl as pretty as you?"

David turned aside. "I am visiting a cousin," he replied. His high voice was awkward and would start to hurt his throat if he kept it up much longer. He took a giant step away from this new stranger.

Unaffected, the man took another stride toward David. "Well, then it becomes my official duty to welcome you to our humble town. I am Sheriff Lustris." The man reached out his arm toward David.

Hannah stopped abruptly a few booths down in the marketplace. She was about to point out the corn husk dolls on a table to David when she noticed he was no longer with them. "Where is David?" she asked Gretchen.

Gretchen also stopped and started to look around anxiously. "He's over there."

"Uh oh." Hannah turned to find him where Gretchen was pointing. "Who is he talking to?"

"That's the local sheriff, Lustris. He's pretty much the most power-ful person out here in this area. This is not good."

Hannah watched David and the sheriff continue. Having former-ly been a waitress in a rough part of town, she was familiar with the body language Lustris was exhibiting. "Is he hitting on David?" Hannah asked in surprise.

"The sheriff's wife is recently deceased," Gretchen explained. "Since then, we have all been avoiding the roaming hands."

"What do you mean by roaming hands?" But she didn't need Gretchen to answer while watching David and the sheriff. "Oh!"

"As sheriff," he continued, "I make a personal effort to make sure the females especially feel safe and comfortable." Lustris wrapped his arm around David's body and put a hand on his back. David tried to turn away, but was caught. He could feel others nearby watching as the man continued. "I would hate for anyone not to enjoy them-selves." He was pressing himself up against David's leg, and his hand was getting lower.

"I think I should go," David squeaked.

"Now, now," the sheriff said, "let's not spoil a good thing." And with that, the sheriff's hand landed on David's behind and gave it a squeeze.

"Enough!" David yelled in his regular voice, as he pushed Sheriff Lustris off of him. "Get off me! What the heck are you doing?" If David thought people were watching before, they definitely were paying attention now.

"Don't get excited, Daphne," Lustris said, as he came at David again. This time David shoved him hard in the shoulder, and the sher-iff backed off.

"This isn't worth it!" David exclaimed, as he unwrapped the fabric from around his head, threw it to the ground, and started to take off the dress. "I'm not a girl, you idiot."

When David was in his regular clothes, revealing himself to be a male, the sheriff stood with his mouth open. The surrounding crowd slowly broke out into boisterous laughter. The sheriff looked around, embarrassed, but quickly became angry.

In all the commotion, David didn't notice Gretchen until she was right next to him. "David, what have you done?"

Lustris snapped his head back to David's direction. "David?" He squinted and analyzed David's face. "Haven't I seen you before?"

"No, sir," Gretchen tried to cover. "This is my cousin. Visiting."

"I was there that day," Lustris said.

Gretchen gripped David's arm, but her voice was calm. "Sir?"

"I saw the tournament. You. You were just a boy then. You are *still* a boy." Lustris stuttered. "You? You! David the Champion is back in Ethelrod?" His confusion drifted away and was replaced with anger about the inciting incident. "You shall pay for this embarrassment, champion or not, *boy*."

"Sheriff, he meant no harm," Gretchen pleaded.

By this time, Hannah had caught up and entered the fray. "David, what's going on?"

The sheriff turned to look at her and jumped back, knocking the table of apples to the ground, the same ones the previous vendor had just finished replacing. Lustris stumbled backward, and the suppressed laughter from the crowd erupted again.

"I'll get you for this," he said, constantly looking back and forth between David and Hannah. "And you, Gretchen, even you for bringing them here."

The sheriff left the marketplace, and everybody went back to their business.

"Okay…what just happened?" Hannah asked.

"The genius here just blew his cover!" Gretchen poked David hard.

"He was hitting on me," David replied. "What was I supposed to do? He felt me up!"

"It won't be long until everyone in Ethelrod knows you're here.

You're not safe, David."

"I'm sorry," David said. "But what was up when he saw Hannah?"

"Men running away scared just by looking at me. That's an ego booster," Hannah joked.

"I don't understand that one," Gretchen answered.

A voice spoke up from nearby. "Well, it's actually very simple." They looked around for its owner. "Down here." It was the fruit vendor, picking up the apples Sheriff Lustris knocked over. All three of them bent down to help him clean up.

"What do you mean?" David asked.

"Well, you know who she looks like, don't you?" he asked Gretchen. They all looked at Hannah.

"Who?" Gretchen asked.

"Your new friend the sheriff's dead wife, of course."

"Really?" Hannah asked.

"What's the big deal?" David didn't understand.

"Not everyone is convinced his wife died of natural causes. She had a big dowry, he had debts, and he was looking for entertainment outside of his marriage already anyway."

"He just got rid of her? He killed his own wife? Who does that?" Gretchen questioned.

"That's the rumor anyway."

"And I just made him an enemy," David added. "Great."

"Way to go, smart guy!" Hannah said.

"We need to get you back to my house immediately," Gretchen said.

Chapter Thirteen

Gretchen was right. It wasn't long before everyone knew of David's return to Ethelrod. The next morning, their day started with a rough knocking on Gretchen's front door. At the entrance stood a knightly looking young man who didn't wait to be asked before coming inside. He wore a shiny metal breastplate with a red cape attached at the shoulders and what looked like shin guards. David noticed the girls gazing at the slight trace of scruff on his strong jawline that matched his dirty-blond hair. A girlish smile spread across Gretchen's face as she silently offered him a seat at the table, which he took. David then detected the sword that hung sheathed at his waist.

No one was talking. The new guest looked around at the three people staring at him. The knight spoke first.

"I am Sir Garrett of the Castle Guard." His voice was strong and authoritative, even though he seemed to be only a few years older than the rest. "I have come to see David the Champion." He turned to the only other male in the room. Relaxed, he said, "Which I assume is you."

David took a step forward. "That's correct."

"I have a note for you from Queen Morgana herself," he stated. The knight handed over a folded yellow piece of parchment with a circle of red sealing wax holding it shut. "Your presence has been requested. You are to come with me immediately."

David broke the hardened wax and read the note. It pretty much said the same thing Sir Garrett had announced, except it was in nice loopy handwriting.

"I don't suppose there's any possibility of refusing?" David asked.

"That would be unwise," Sir Garrett assured him.

David noticed Sir Garrett's hand grip the hilt of his sword as he said it. David looked back up, and their eyes met. The knight quickly released the sword.

"A request from the queen seldom goes unanswered. One way or another, I'm sure she could get you to see her," Sir Garrett replied.

"Then I guess I'm going," David replied. "Right now?"

"Immediately," Sir Garrett nodded.

David looked back at Hannah and Gretchen, who instead of looking at him were staring at Sir Garrett. "It doesn't say anything about bringing guests, does it?" David asked. That got the girls' attention.

"Excuse me?"

"Well," David explained, "it doesn't say I have to come alone. I'm bringing Gretchen and Hannah with me, or I'm not coming at all."

Sir Garrett looked from David to the girls and back to David. "I guess it doesn't say you can't. But I only brought two horses with me for the ride back."

"We could share!"

The shouting came out of nowhere. Both girls had instantly jumped at the chance to be the first to make this suggestion. Eventually, Gretchen won the chance to ride with Sir Garrett, and Hannah was stuck with David.

"What do you mean 'stuck' with me?" David asked.

"Oh, nothing," Hannah replied, sounding embarrassed. "It's nothing."

"Don't worry about it, lad," Sir Garrett said, as he clapped David on the shoulder. "There are many women in the city who are excited to meet you."

Hannah sniffed at this. *Disapproval?*

David started to smile but got distracted by a key word. *Lad? Why is everyone around here so obsessed with my age? Wasn't it just a few months ago that I was the champion who had a chance at marrying a princess?* Correction, a few years ago. Coming back to Ethelrod was more of an adjustment than David had expected.

"Shall we go?" David asked. They all made a move toward the door on their way to the royal reception waiting for them in the kingdom.

"Wait," Gretchen stopped them. "We can't go dressed like this!"

David was given a mail shirt, similar to the one he wore when he fought in the contest. He was also given a nice green cloth tunic to wear over it. He did choose to stick with his jeans and sneakers, though. After what seemed like way too much time, and too much awkward silence between Sir Garrett and David, the girls finally emerged. Gretchen appeared in a cream floor-length gown with a lot of flowery embroidery sewn into the fabric. Her previous braids were replaced with thick curls that cascaded around her shoulders. Sir Garrett's mouth was open, but he quickly shut it.

If David thought Gretchen was pretty, all thoughts were erased when Hannah entered the room. She wore a deep purple dress with long flowing sleeves. There was gold-colored thread detailing the edges of the hem, cuffs, and neckline. Her dark, sleek hair was in a half-up, half-down style. Even though David didn't know what to call it, he liked it. More importantly, he liked her with it. She walked toward him and he began to smile instinctively.

"You look, um, nice," he stumbled.

"Tunic with jeans and sneakers. Decent combo. I like it." Hannah lifted up the skirt on her hem and showed off her Converse.

"Perfect," David replied. "I guess we think alike."

Sir Garrett looked around the room and nodded with general approval of the now-presentable trio. "Shall we?"

Chapter Fourteen

Gretchen rode on the back of Sir Garrett's horse in a graceful sidesaddle position, while Hannah awkwardly straddled the horse behind David. It took a while, but eventually they made it to the woods of Ethelrod where David had arrived the first time. The forest was thicker than David remembered. The dense, intertwining branches and leaves also made the forest darker than his memory recalled.

"We just need to make it through the woods and we'll be at the main kingdom. Is that right, Sir Garrett?" David asked.

Sir Garrett rode in front of David and didn't respond. *Can't he hear me?* David decided to try again, louder this time. "Sir Garrett?" Still nothing, but Gretchen had turned back.

This time Gretchen jabbed the knight in the side. "Sir *Garrett,*" she said, strongly emphasizing the last part. That got his attention. "David asked you a question."

"Oh, sorry, David," Sir Garrett apologized. "You have to forgive me. I'm not actually used to this new name yet."

"What do you mean?" Hannah asked.

Sir Garrett pulled his horse back to be side by side with David and Hannah. "You see," he explained, "David and I have a lot more in common than you think. Recently, I also won a contest. I was not always a knight. Queen Morgana's father, while he still ruled, hosted a tournament that offered a spot in the Castle Guard for the winner. I am the son of a blacksmith, who had always dreamt of becoming a knight, so I decided to leave everything at home behind to compete. And I mean everything." Did David catch a glance back at Gretchen? "And as it happens, I ended up winning the tournament and my knighthood as a member of the Castle Guard. So you see, I am not really used to being called Sir Garrett yet. If you don't mind, I think Garrett will be just fine with me for now." Garrett seemed a little more relaxed being able to drop the "sir" for a moment.

"Sure thing, Garrett," David replied. He knew Garrett wasn't that much older, but for some reason it still felt like calling a teacher by his first name for the first time.

"How long ago was this contest?" Hannah asked.

"Ten years, same as David. But it was only recently that I came of age to claim my prize."

"You must have been just a boy!" Hannah said amazed. "What did you do?"

"A story for another time perhaps," Garrett avoided. "What were you asking me before?"

"Oh, yeah," David replied. "We should be right there as soon as we leave the forest, correct?"

"That's true, but we still have a few more hours before—"

Just then Garrett jumped off his horse and tackled David and Hannah to the ground. David had the wind knocked out of him, so he couldn't yell at Garrett, wanting to know what the heck was going on. He found the answer himself: a dagger was stuck into the trunk of a tree nearby. He quickly turned in the opposite direction and saw three menacing men standing on the path behind them.

Garrett quickly got up and ran to Gretchen, who was still on Garrett's horse. "Isn't that…" he started to ask.

"Balthazar and some of his men," Gretchen finished. "Yes."

The men watched as David helped Hannah to her feet.

Garrett continued to whisper to Gretchen, just loud enough that David could still hear. "I thought Lustris caught him and locked him up for good after robbing and murdering all those men on the Western Shore."

"He did," she answered. "I don't understand how he could be here." Her hands fumbled nervously with the reins.

"Well, he couldn't have just walked out of his prison cell."

"You're right." Gretchen's face showed she was thinking hard. "Unless…Oh, my God…David!" She looked at him with fright, causing Hannah to grab David's arm with both hands.

Balthazar, the larger man in the middle with a gruff bearded face and tattered clothes, called out to them in a booming rough voice. "We are here for the Champion! Hand him over!"

"David," Gretchen said, "Lustris must have released him and sent him after you."

David was speechless, as he looked between the three men and his friends. "Well, that doesn't seem fair for what happened in the town square. Are you sure he would overreact this much?"

"Absolutely. This is Lustris."

Balthazar was done with their whispering and done waiting. "If you don't hand him over, we'll just take his life and yours at the same time!"

Garrett went over to his saddle and untied an extra sword. He threw it to David. "I trust you remember how to use this?"

"Like riding a bike," David answered.

"A what?"

"Never mind."

"Get Hannah on that horse," Garrett commanded. David helped her up and heard Garrett give instructions to Gretchen. "I need you and Hannah to get out of here. Just keep riding."

"No way!" Hannah objected, looking down at David. "We're not going anywhere."

"Garrett, you might need our help," Gretchen pleaded.

"That is not happening. You need to go. Now!" Garrett yelled.

"Garrett…"

Garrett didn't wait for the girls to agree as he slapped the backside of the horses hard. The animals sped off into the forest. Garrett pulled out his sword and stared at David. "You ready?"

"As much as I'll ever be." David took out his sword as well and threw its sheath aside. *I hope I remember how to do this.* They both faced the men down the path.

Balthazar yelled down to them. "You don't have to die, too, young knight. Run away like a little boy, while you still have the chance."

"You will pay for your crimes with your life, Balthazar," Garrett retorted confidently. This made David feel stronger. He also felt oddly comforted that he wasn't the only one being picked on for his age, finally.

Younger people can do big things, too, he thought.

David believed Garrett's and his teamwork would get them through this. It had to. A question sparked in David's brain.

Are you allowed to die on an adventure in a different world? David wasn't sure there was exactly a rule against it. He became determined not to find out.

The same time that David and Garrett started running forward, two of Balthazar's men came sprinting toward them, screaming a battle cry. The one on the left threw a dagger at Garrett, but he knocked it aside with his sword like he was playing baseball. Garrett ran at his assailant, spun the opponent's sword out of his hand with a clockwise twisting motion, and smashed the hilt of his sword into the guy's forehead. The man fell to the ground, and Garrett continued on to Balthazar.

David's attacker came at him fast. David slid to his right just in time to miss a sharp blow and run past him. They spun around quickly and their swords met in the air with a loud clang. More clanging behind him told David that Garrett was already with Balthazar, but David had to concentrate on this guy first. The opponent kept slashing at David and grunting with every swing. David did a good enough job circling, keeping out of range, and using his sword to block any attempts that came too close. He remembered the book from Mr. Linden's library about sword fighting. He used what he could about defensive stances and maneuvers. He hadn't finished the book, though, and never made it to the chapter on offense.

David kept backing away, and his assailant started to laugh. "Is baby too scared to fight?"

Breathing in deeply, he took a strong step forward and swung his sword across his body. It hit the other sword hard and knocked it from his opponent's unsuspecting hands.

David was now the one smiling while the other looked scared. However, the fight was not over yet. The assailant reached behind him and pulled out a bow and an arrow from a quiver on his back. David knew if this guy had time to nock the arrow in the bow, he was dead. He starting swinging his sword faster, making his opponent move around frantically, unable to set his arrow properly in the bow. When David took a step too close, the man slashed at him with the arrow. The cut to his arm stung and started to bleed. David grabbed his arm and backed up. The assailant came forward quickly, locked an edge of his bow behind David's ankle, and pulled. David tripped and fell onto his back, looking up at the man who now had the arrow loaded and aimed down at his face.

David's sword was out of reach. There was not much he could do.

David's attacker smiled down with crooked yellow teeth. "I'll be the one known for killing the famous Champion. I'll bet there's even some money in it for me, too."

In a last attempt, David did something he had also read about before. This time it was in a comic strip. With all the strength he could muster, he lifted his leg fast and hard until his foot came in contact with the man's crotch. He screamed and doubled over in pain, dropping his bow and arrow and falling to the ground. David scrambled to his sword, rolled back to his attacker, and slammed the handle of his sword onto the side of the man's head as he had seen Garrett do.

Balthazar had Garrett's throat in one hand and a sword raised in his other. David screamed out just in time. "Hey!"

Balthazar stopped mid-swing and looked toward David.

"Leave him alone. I'm the one you want."

Balthazar nodded and smiled. "Okay, then." He lifted Garrett with one hand and gave him a huge head-butt before throwing Garrett's limp body to the side. "I was excited to be released on the condition that I had to remove someone. And when I found out it was a kid, it was just too hard to say no."

Balthazar walked toward David, and David gripped his sword, ready to fight.

"This isn't a game, kid. No silly tournament with loopholes to save you this time," Balthazar taunted.

"Are you going to talk all the time or are we going to finish this?"

"As you wish."

And with that, Balthazar came at David, who ducked just in time to miss a running swing at his head. David took a downward swing, but missed. A surprisingly forceful backhand from Balthazar across his face knocked him down. David's sword fell from his hand to the ground. David looked up at Balthazar, who had his sword on his shoulder, waiting.

"Go on," he said. "Go pick it up."

David got his sword and stood up. This time he raced at Balthazar. His blow was blocked, and once again Balthazar knocked him to the ground with a fist that felt like a sledgehammer. This time Balthazar offered no second chances.

David could hardly breathe because of how many times he had been recently knocked around. Balthazar's wicked smile both scared David and told him this was the end. Balthazar looked at his sword. "It would be over too quickly if I used this," he said. He threw his sword to the side and reached down toward David. "It's better to watch the life slowly leave the body."

David couldn't move before Balthazar's hands were locked on his throat, blocking all air from entering his lungs. David tried to claw at

Balthazar's face, but he couldn't reach. He gripped Balthazar's wrists, trying to pull them from his throat, but David felt himself getting tired. His lungs were burning. David's legs kept kicking and thrashing, but they made no contact. Balthazar's face was starting to get blurry.

"This is everything I was hoping for and more," grumbled Balthazar.

Suddenly, Balthazar's face twisted into pained confusion. The grip on David's throat lessened only a bit. He took in a quick gulp of air, and his vision steadied. David looked around and saw that Balthazar's chest had begun to sprout feathers that leaked a dark red liquid. Watching, another sprout blossomed and the grip on David's throat was released. Balthazar's body crumpled down on top of him. David coughed hard, allowing much needed air to refill his lungs. He looked at Balthazar's body that lay unmoving on his legs. David pushed himself free and saw that the feathery sprouts were actually arrows in his chest.

David saw her down the path with the second attacker's previously discarded bow in her hands. She was the one who shot the arrows that killed Balthazar. Hannah had just saved David's life.

Gretchen gently revived Garrett, and David went to take the bow from an obviously shaken Hannah.

"Are you okay?" he asked.

"I just killed someone," she replied without looking at him.

David slowly slipped the bow out of her fingers. "You saved my life."

Hannah turned to David. "I'm glad you're okay." She wrapped her arms around him and laid her head on his shoulder. "But I don't like how it had to happen."

"It'll be okay," David assured her. "I'm sorry it had to be you, but it will be okay." He pushed her back so he could see her face. "You did nothing wrong. You hear me? If you think about it, you did a very good thing."

"You're right," Hannah agreed. "But I don't have to like it." She glanced toward the path and a small smile came back to her lips. "Besides," she continued, "it looks like some people are having enough fun for the both of us."

David followed the direction of Hannah's gaze and found Gretchen's and Garrett's lips locked as they embraced. David felt weird and uncomfortable and didn't know how to interrupt the moment or even if he should. He coughed loudly, and the couple snapped back to reality, both wiping their lips in an attempt to erase the moment.

"What's going on here?" David joked.

Gretchen and Garrett turned, laughing and still holding hands. "I told you I was a blacksmith's son who left everything to become a knight. I only half-expected I would win the tournament. I had to leave the people I cared most about behind. But what I didn't tell you—"

Gretchen finished for him, "was that Garrett and I are from the same village. His father works right down the street from us. Neither of us had officially confessed our feelings for each other, and then he just left. I didn't know how he felt for me until—"

"Until just now, I guess," Garrett said. The couple looked at each other, smiled, and squeezed each other's hands affectionately.

"Awwww," Hannah sighed, as she leaned into David.

Not knowing why, David awkwardly withdrew. "Shouldn't we continue on?"

Garrett quickly refocused and agreed. "Can't keep the queen waiting!"

Chapter Fifteen

The ride through the forest was peacefully uneventful after that. At one point, they came to a clearing that Gretchen pointed out to David as the first place they met.

"Right here?" Hannah asked.

"Well, actually it was up there," Gretchen corrected. She pointed up high into the trees.

"All the way up—" Hannah stopped. "Is that a—"

"Yep!" David finished. "That is indeed one of your father's couches in a tree."

David saw how the surrounding branches had started to grow around the couch. It really proved how long he had been gone if a grown-up Gretchen hadn't already.

"That's weird," Hannah said.

It was only a little farther from that point until David laid eyes on another familiar sight. The forest ended and opened up into a huge grassy field. On the other side of that field was the high kingdom of Ethelrod.

The passage through town was similar to David's first visit, only this time he was on a horse. The streets were busy with people and merchants, and everyone they got close to stopped what they were doing and stared until they had passed. They weaved their way through the crowded streets to the town square and the great wall on the north side that held the front gate to the castle.

Garrett announced himself as Sir Garrett of the Castle Guard. "I have brought David the Champion and some guests to be received at the request of the queen." That was enough for the men on the other side. They raised the gate for all four of them to pass through and then closed the gate behind them.

A curving path led them through the outer boundary of the fortress into the main courtyard. It was busy with activity from people of several different ways of life. More elegantly dressed folks were coming and going, while the plainer, seemingly lower-class people were working transporting goods, dealing with horses, and doing other jobs. The four of them rode right up to the front steps of the castle, where attendants came to take their horses. Garrett hopped off and offered Gretchen a hand to help her down. David did the same for Hannah.

"From here," Garrett explained, "we will go inside and be escorted to the Great Hall. There you will see the queen and her court, and we can finally see what this is all about."

"You think it might be more than just a friendly reunion for old time's sake?" David asked.

"We will find out."

The Great Hall was at the end of a complex system of hallways and staircases. It was enormous. High vaulted ceilings were supported by tall carved pillars. The stained glass windows let in bright streams of colored light that streaked the floor where numerous fine-looking court members were socializing. Garrett guided them through the crowd to the small opening in front of the throne where Queen Morgana sat.

Morgana had changed a lot since David had last seen her. Yes, she was now queen, but there was no evidence that the last ten years had been especially kind to her. She wore rich clothing, but it seemed slanted on her, like it didn't fit or everything just needed a tug in a different direction. Her face was blank and her eyes were glossy. Her hair was starting to go gray and pieces of it rebelled and stuck apart from whatever sloppy hairdo she had styled. David tried to think what could have happened to the gentle woman ten years ago who convinced David to fight for her right to marry a man she chose and loved. Then he remembered what Gretchen told him earlier. He figured being surrounded by that much death and abandonment could definitely have an adverse effect on anyone.

Close behind her was a man standing strong and upright. While Morgana's gaze was at the floor as she sat with her chin in her hand, this man was constantly surveying the hall. His long, dark hair was slicked back. He also had a dark beard and eyebrows. One eyebrow didn't match due to a scar that interrupted it. A thin pink line went from his forehead, down over his eye, and ended on his left cheek. In his constant watch over the crowd, he noticed the four visitors getting closer, and his eyes locked on David. It was then that David noticed one eye was dark and the other eye, the eye with the scar, was an unsettling blue-gray.

Morgana finally looked up and started jumping with excitement in her seat on the throne. "Oh, they've come! They've come!" she said through giggles.

Garrett stepped forward and got down on one knee. "My queen, may I present David the Champion and his guests, Gretchen of the Western Shore, and, Hannah, who also comes from David's world." Gretchen curtsied and Hannah copied her. David bowed.

"Of course! I know who it is!" Morgana snapped. That wasn't how David remembered her at all. She then became pleasant again, almost flirty. "Hello, David." She looked him up and down, smiling widely.

"Hello, Queen Morgana," David replied. "It has been a while since we have seen each other."

"Yes, it has," Morgana agreed. "But you don't look like you've aged a day. How curious and wonderful. Isn't it wonderful, Valstayne?" She motioned toward the man behind her, who only nodded. "Oh, you haven't met my most trusted advisor. This is Lord Valstayne." They both inclined their heads toward the other.

"And who is this you have brought with you?" Morgana asked.

"My friend Hannah."

"Are you two engaged or married?"

David wasn't expecting this question and stumbled over his response. "Ah, no, your highness."

Morgana stared at David for a moment and slowly a word came through her lips. "Perfect." She then addressed the rest of the room. "Get out! David and I must speak in private, and I wish to be left alone!" The courtiers made their way to the door as ordered. "Valstayne, you are to stay, of course," Morgana added.

"And may it please your queen," David started, "I should like at least Hannah to stay as well."

Hannah was at his side, whispering. "David, I don't know…"

"It won't please me," Morgana said, "but she may stay if you like."

David looked for approval from Garrett and Gretchen. "Gretchen and I will wait for you at the gate. Meet us there, if you can, when you are finished." He started to escort Gretchen out, but then he turned back. "And David, just make sure she stays happy. She is not the same woman you knew."

When the room was cleared, only David, Hannah, Queen Morgana, and Lord Valstayne remained.

"David, I'm sure you're wondering why I have called you here." She didn't wait for a reply from him. "I must admit I was very excited to hear you had returned. You left rather quickly before, and no one knew where you had gone. It seems as though you always appear in my hour of need. Sadly, you do not know of what has been going on since then. You do not know about my curse."

"Your curse?" David asked.

"My queen…" Lord Valstayne began.

Is he trying to stop the conversation?

"I am cursed, Valstayne!" Morgana snapped again. "Please explain to me how every man I love or at least choose to marry ends up dead? It even sometimes affects the ones I only consider. If this is not a curse, I don't know what is."

"Yes, my queen," Valstayne appeased.

"Which is why I have called you here, David," she smiled. "David the Champion."

"I'm afraid I don't understand," David said.

"Don't you see? You and I are going to be married."

David looked at Hannah quickly and he was sure the horror he saw on Hannah's face matched the shock on his own. He tried to compose himself.

Morgana continued. "Oh, no, it's perfect. You are the one who gave me the right to choose my own husband. It is fitting you be that husband now. And look at you, still young and preserved, just like the day I met you. Surely, you won't die on me."

David had no idea what to say. Hannah was quiet and no help either. He struggled for a response. "I am not sure," he explained, "that I am worthy of such an, er, honor."

"Silliness!" Morgana replied. "You are still loved as David the Champion. You will give me back the support I need."

"Support?"

"There are those who say I should be doing more to stop these wars between the lords fighting for my affection. Those who say I have lost my touch…and my mind. They go as far to say that I should not even be queen! Ha! That will change when I finally marry you. It will all be better when we are married." She turned to Valstayne. "It must happen immediately."

"I do not think—" he started.

"Immediately, Valstayne!" Morgana shrieked. Then, she quickly changed her face into a pleasant but creepy smile. "How does tomorrow sound, David?"

Valstayne answered for him. "It must be at least a week to prepare and get things in order." The man glared at David. David could feel the hatred burning through his different-colored eyes.

"Fine, fine, fine," Morgana waved her hand like her wedding was a trivial matter. "What do you say to my proposal, David?"

David was silent. The surprise of all this was just too much. *Agree to be married to a bipolar queen in a fantasy land? What was the polite way to say, "No way in hell"?*

Hannah came close to David and whispered in his ear. "Remember what Garrett said," she reminded him. "Just make her happy. Who knows what will happen if you refuse her?" David couldn't believe what he was hearing. He was about to object when Hannah's soft hand on his arm calmed him down. "Say yes now and we can find a way out of it later." David nodded.

"I graciously accept your offer, Morgana."

The queen squealed in delight and kicked her feet back and forth like a little girl. Valstayne had the opposite reaction that only showed in his eyes and tightening jaw muscles. "My soothsayer," Morgana said, "has come up with a potion using lizard eyes that she swears will protect my loved ones. I will have some sent to you as soon as possible." She got off her throne and walked over to David. She put her hand on his face and slowly caressed it. "You won't die on me, will you?"

David gulped. "I will do my best."

"Wonderful!" And with that, she rose and swayed as she left her throne, humming her way out of the Great Hall. David and Hannah stood alone with Lord Valstayne. He walked toward them with his hands folded behind his back.

"Let's keep this between ourselves, shall we?" Lord Valstayne hissed his "s" sounds and each one gave David shivers down his spine. "We wouldn't want anything to happen to you now, would we?" Lord Valstayne's voice was more threatening than concerned.

"What do you mean?" Hannah asked.

"It's a dangerous world these days. Who knows if some accident or fatal attack might come your way? Eh, David?"

Was that meant to be a friendly warning?

Valstayne continued. "You should watch your back before someone puts a knife in it."

Nope, definitely a threat.

Lord Valstayne left David and Hannah. Hannah quickly started pacing in short bursts across the stone floor of the Great Hall.

"Oh, my God, David!"

"Okay, okay. We'll think of something." He tried to assure her, but he couldn't even convince himself.

"This is what Gretchen warned us about. Now when people find out you are actually engaged to Morgana, *everyone* will want you dead instead of just some."

"So we do what Valstayne said. We don't tell anyone. No one will find out."

"And you trust that creep?"

The truth was that he didn't. If anything, Valstayne was the number one person to watch out for at the moment.

"And Morgana," Hannah continued, "she should definitely *not* be ruling Ethelrod. Not if all of this is true. She's letting her country rip itself apart and not lifting a finger. Not to mention—she's insane! There is seriously something wrong with that woman. What do you think?"

David didn't know what to think. Pretty soon everyone would be out to get him, and he could barely handle just having Lustris against him.

"We need to get back to Garrett and Gretchen. Maybe they'll have some ideas."

Chapter Sixteen

David and Hannah left the Great Hall and went to meet Garrett and Gretchen at the front gate. The part of the castle they were in had been abandoned. They tried to find their way back by memory. Eventually, they came to a landing where two staircases would take them in different directions.

"I think it's the right one," David suggested.

"I'm pretty sure it's the left one."

"No," David argued. "It's the right. Let's go." Hannah followed.

The staircase led them far down into the castle, deeper than they should have gone. David didn't want to admit he had chosen the wrong way, so he refused to acknowledge that they were lost. They came to a dark, empty hallway with no signs of life.

"All right, let's turn back," David said, defeated.

"Wait." Hannah pointed to some sort of flickering light coming from under a door a little ways down the hall. "Maybe there's someone down here who can help us find our way out."

They walked to the door that was damp and smelled like it was rotting. They slowly opened the door, and it creaked like it was about to fall apart any second.

Inside, the room was dimly lit, but they could still make out the stacks of papers and books that lined the floor, tables, and shelves. There wasn't much space that wasn't covered. Some piles on the floor went all the way to the ceiling. There was a small maze through the papers that they tried to follow toward the light. They hit a dead end here and there, but they eventually found the candle on the table that was the light source. They were startled when they also found an old man sitting at the desk, staring at them.

He wore a solid brown robe like that of a monk. He was mostly bald on the top of his head, except for a few wispy white hairs. He was looking at them, but not moving. Was he okay?

"I know you are here," he finally said in a frail voice. "I heard you open the door and tiptoe through the stacks. I can hear you breathing now, and I won't mention anything about how you smell. That would be rude."

David noticed the man's milky eyes, staring a little bit to the side of them. This man was blind.

"We're sorry, sir," Hannah apologized. The man's head turned in their direction. "We were lost and hoping to find a way out. After the day we've had, we just want to go home."

"It sounds like you've had a difficult time."

"We were almost killed on our way here and now we have to deal with a crazy, incompetent queen!" Hannah blurted. David tried quickly to shush her, but it was too late.

"It's all right, boy," the man said. "You may speak freely here."

"Who are you?" David asked suspiciously. He was not totally ready to trust a stranger yet, especially one found in the dungeons.

"I could ask you the same question! However, it seems you have asked first," the man conceded. "I am Riordan, High Historian of Ethelrod and Keeper of Records. Even without my sight, I have been responsible for listening and dictating all of Ethelrod's history to my assistant."

"I'm Hannah," Hannah replied. "And this is David."

"Not David the Champion?" Riordan asked.

"The same," David admitted.

"Well, it doesn't take sight for me to guess why you have come here.

Am I correct in guessing you are the latest in line to marry the queen?"

"I shouldn't tell you whether or not I am."

"Smart. You'd be a perfect specimen for Morgana. I'm sure she has already given you several reasons why." He grunted. "I have already added too many death certificates to my records because of Morgana and her marriage predicament."

"Then you know what we're dealing with!" Hannah said. "That woman should not be in charge of anything."

"There are many of us who agree," Riordan replied. "Sadly, there is not much we can do."

David liked the use of "us" and "we" and began to trust Riordan a little more. "Is there any way out of this?"

"Out of your marriage?" Riordan asked. "The easiest way would be to run back to where you came from and never return. However, all that does is leave Ethelrod alone with no chance of a bright future anytime soon."

"What do you mean where we came from?" David asked.

"Well, I am assuming you are not from this world, correct?"

"How do you know that?" Hannah wondered.

"David the Champion. He comes for a day, changes the path of Ethelrod, and disappears for ten years. We have had a visitor like you before. The only option is that you are like that visitor, and you do not belong here. I am the High Historian; it is my job to know these things and make the connections."

"You've had another visitor before David?" Hannah questioned. David knew she was thinking of her father.

"Oh, yes," Riordan answered. "And he made quite a surprising impact on Ethelrod's path as well. David, have you ever wondered why all visitors were required to fight in a contest to the death?"

"Not particularly, I guess."

"It is because the last visitor stole the greatest hope Ethelrod ever had of reaching a truly Golden Age."

"What happened?" Hannah asked.

I would be curious, too, if my dad had a secret past I didn't know about, David thought.

"It's a long story and one that has been forgotten by everyone. It is time people remembered."

"Please tell us," Hannah begged.

"It was centuries ago," he began. "By chance, two children of warring families had ended up falling in love. Instead of trying to conquer each other for power, the young couple's love inspired the enemies to combine their families and estates peacefully through marriage. A unified Ethelrod was in creation. They were set to be married when they turned eighteen, but they never reached their wedding day."

"What happened?" David asked.

"It is rumored that a strange, young gentleman came from another world. No one knew much about him. He kept to himself and his only friendship was formed with the engaged couple. This is when things turned dark. One day, the young couple went out with the strange visitor and never returned. Search parties were sent to retrieve them, but they came back with nothing. It was finally declared that the visitor had kidnapped them and a reward was put out for the man, dead or alive."

"Then what?" Hannah asked.

"At this time, the people had become very happy with the expectation of a united kingdom and wouldn't allow the two families to continue fighting for power again. By popular demand, a neutral party was elected to fill in as steward for the kingdom until the rightful heirs returned. Seeing as they never returned, gradually over the centuries, the people forgot about the missing rulers and acknowledged this new family, the family of Morgana and her father, as the rightful rulers. In the beginning, their position was to merely keep the peace until their time was up.

"They gradually started to abuse their power and steal from their own subjects. By this time, there was nothing anyone could do. No one remembered who the rulers were they had been waiting for, or the visitor who had taken them, or even the reason they had the tradition of forcing visitors into a contest to the death."

"How do you know all this?" David questioned.

"I only know the story because my assistant and I stumbled upon some ancient documents lost in time. And now, four people know the story."

"The reason this land is tearing itself apart is because Morgana's ancestors were put in power after a visitor kidnapped the young couple and heirs to the throne," David summarized.

"Or they left with him," Hannah defended.

"No one can say for sure," Riordan mediated. "But it can be agreed that the visitor's actions set Ethelrod on this path. And only ten years ago another visitor came to push us farther down this road."

David felt the sting of guilt with that last part. It was partly his fault that Morgana's rule had become so disastrous. And now he was expected to marry her; that is if he could survive. He thought hard. "Riordan, you made it seem that going home and never coming back was only one option to get out of this mess."

"You are correct. Should you wish to help, there is another solution that is going to be more difficult."

"What is it?" Hannah asked.

"You have to go home, and—" Riordan said.

"I don't understand," David interrupted. "How can that—"

"We have to find the missing heirs in our own world," Hannah finished.

"Correct," Riordan agreed. "It seems impossible to think that you could find them. But if you do and are able to bring them back to Ethelrod, they could take their place as rightful king and queen of Ethelrod, ending Morgana's reign."

"Piece of cake," David joked bitterly. "All we have to do is find two people out of six billion! We'll be back in no time."

Riordan let out a long sigh. "Then it may be another few centuries before things are set right."

"Not exactly," Hannah said.

"You know how to find the needle in the haystack?" Riordan scoffed.

"Well, I don't, but we know someone who can. We know the visitor."

Riordan sat up straight at this news. "And you think he would tell you the whereabouts of Ethelrod's missing heirs?"

"I think so. He's my father," Hannah confessed.

Riordan's hands went crazy motioning for them to leave. "Then go! Be gone! I don't know how you do it, but you must return home as quickly as you can. Find the heirs and return with them. The future peace of Ethelrod is in your hands. What are you waiting for? Get out of here!"

"How do we get back to the front gate?" Hannah asked, embarrassed.

Riordan told them.

"I'm really glad we met you," David admitted.

"Don't you remember, champion? We have met before." Riordan lifted up the bottom of his robe and revealed a large healed gash on his leg. "Remember?" There was something familiar about it.

"The warrior from the tournament! That was you?" David asked amazed.

"You saved my life so I could tell you how to save us all." Riordan smiled and lowered his robe back down. "Now go!"

Chapter Seventeen

David and Hannah found Garrett and Gretchen waiting at the front gate. They mounted their horses, and David made sure they rode out of the kingdom as soon as possible. The ride back to Gretchen's village was shorter, without any interruptions from murderous robbers, but there was still time for David and Hannah to alternate telling what they had learned since they separated. Gretchen became worried at the fact that David's wedding proposal now made him a prime target.

"No, this is great!" Garrett exclaimed. "Ethelrod finally has a chance for peace if we can restore these ancient rulers to the throne. We have to get you home as soon as possible."

"All we have to do is close the book, and Hannah and I can return home," David said.

"That's all?" Garrett asked.

"It's that simple. I've seen him do it before," Gretchen explained.

"And we'll have to be super quick," Hannah added. "A week at home is like a year here."

"We would appreciate the speed," Garrett joked.

"All right," David said. "Let's go inside and get that book!"

When Gretchen opened the door to her home, her face went blank and empty. They walked inside and found the entire place ransacked. Tables were overturned and a chair lay shattered in the middle of the floor. David instinctively ran over the rubble to the wardrobe and swung open the doors. "The book!" he exclaimed. "It's gone!"

"What are we going to do?" Hannah worried.

"Who could have done this?" Garrett asked.

Gretchen just stood silently, looking at her destroyed home.

A voice surprised them. "I know who did it." They all turned to see the apple vendor from the previous day at the front door. "It was Sheriff Lustris."

Hannah started to freak out. "Lustris stole the book? David, what are we going to do?"

"I've had enough of this jerk. I'm going to go right over there and take it back with this." David drew his sword and marched toward the door. Garrett grabbed him and blocked his exit. "Let go of me, Garrett!"

"I understand what you're feeling," Garrett reasoned. "But this cannot be the way to go about things. Lustris has a fortress and guards, and he is not a bad fighter himself."

David threw Garrett's arms off of him forcefully. "Then what do you propose we do, Sir Garrett? Any bright ideas in that suit of armor of yours?"

"We can't go straight at him," Garrett explained. "It's much too risky. This is the man who originally captured Balthazar."

"And he's the man who sent him after me."

"And supposedly murdered his wife," Gretchen added.

"Oh, I forgot about that," Hannah said sadly.

"Since we can't go after him directly, we need to think of something else," Garrett said. "We can't just go running at him. We need a plan."

"You could get him when he's alone." The four of them turned once again to the apple vendor still at the door. "He is always alone for a drink right before he goes to bed. Every night like clockwork, he gets drunk."

"But we couldn't go right for the book," David figured. "We'll need something to get him away from the book so we can take it."

"Like a distraction?" Gretchen chimed in.

"Exactly."

"Sounds like a start," Garrett agreed.

"How do you know all of this?" Hannah asked the vendor.

"I used to work for the man before he fired me."

"Is that also how you know so much about what happened to his wife?" The vendor nodded. Hannah asked, "How much do I really look like her?"

"Mirror image, Miss."

"And how far away do you think the sheriff needs to get before we can look for what he stole?"

"If you could get him to the barn, that would probably be safe," he reckoned.

"What are you thinking, Hannah?" David asked.

"I have an idea," Hannah replied. "Garrett, your dad is a blacksmith. Do you think he has any chains we could borrow?"

"Of course."

A sly grin spread across Hannah's face. "Okay, everyone, listen up! Here's what we are going to do."

Hannah never believed her expertise in fake hauntings would eventually pay off like this. They didn't have any dry ice, but the barn looked fantastic. This was going to go above and beyond anything she had ever tried before.

The elaborate set-up Hannah instructed took much longer to complete than expected. Lucky for the group, Lustris was still drinking well into the early morning hours. David and Garrett were crouched in the bushes outside the window, waiting for Hannah. She came running up in one of Gretchen's simple white nightgowns.

"Gretchen and I are done in the barn," she announced. "Is he still drinking?"

"Like a fish," Garrett commented.

"Are we ready?" David asked.

"Everything is all set," Hannah confirmed.

"Are you sure you want to go through with this?" he questioned.

"What could possibly go wrong?" Hannah stood at the window and gave a signal. "Go for it!"

Both of the boys began rattling their chains together. Looking back, the last time she took a bold risk, she got caught, and it cost her. She hoped this time would have a more profitable result. It had to. This time her plan included being seen and relying on her likeness to the person she was attempting to imitate. If only Lustris would look up from his glass!

"Louder," she whispered.

They shook the chains louder. Lustris sloppily looked toward his window and then away again. His neck snapped his head back, and he dropped his cup to the floor.

"Got him."

Hannah stepped backward, and Lustris followed her, dumbstruck, to the window. She turned and walked across the lawn toward the softly glowing barn entrance. Lustris ran to the back door and banged it open. He stumbled as fast as he could after her. Hannah quickened her pace.

Gretchen had just finished the last of the preparations as Hannah made it to the large barn door. She winked at Hannah before hiding behind a bale of hay. Hannah stood in the middle of the barn and waited for Lustris to appear. She could hear his stumbling and panting from chasing her down the lawn. He came into view at the barn door and instantly his eyes and mouth opened in awe. Lustris dropped to his knees in disbelief.

On almost every surface they could find, white candles were placed and lit. The candles dripped their wax down the sides of the walls, the partitions for the animals, the rafters, and the edges of the hay loft. Hannah was surrounded by the brilliant light of all the tiny flames. It was an amazing sight to see, but she could tell Lustris was horrified.

"I know what you did to me!" Hannah bellowed, a little impressed with herself.

Lustris shook his head and moved his mouth, but no words came out.

"How could you? I was your wife!"

His head went into his hands between his knees, and Lustris started to sob. He looked up at Hannah with tears running down his face. Hannah slowly raised her arm and pointed a finger at him. He tried to hide in his hands again. The sobbing grew louder. "Murderer!" she screamed. "You will burn for this crime."

"No!" Lustris yelled. He withdrew his face from the ground. His sad, pained, and tortured face was now one of complete rage. "You don't tell me what to do. I killed you the last time you gave me instructions." He got to his feet, stumbling back and forth shakily, and pulled out a dagger. "I killed you once, and I can kill you again!"

Lustris stormed into the barn after Hannah. This was not part of the plan. She retreated into the barn and wove between the partitions, but he followed closely. He swung his dagger around for a piece of her, and she kept out of reach, but only just barely. He got angrier and started throwing his weight around more. Lustris knocked into the walls and partitions. Candles fell to the floor at their feet. Lustris was between her and the barn door, so Hannah frantically looked around for another way out. She found a ladder that led to the hay loft, ran to it, and started to climb. Lustris kept on her trail with loathing in his eyes.

"Our turn!" David told Garrett, as he watched Lustris exit. They entered the house through the open back door to search for the stolen book.

David and Garrett had searched the entire first floor with no luck.

"It's got to be here somewhere," David said frustrated. "We are wasting time." He tried to think. "Does the sheriff have any type of trophy room or something?"

"No," Garrett replied, "but he does have a hunting room. Let's go upstairs."

They climbed the steps and ran to a room at the end of the hall. David opened the door to find a room littered with more animals and animal parts than a zoo. Skin rugs lined the floor, while mounted heads and antlers covered the walls. This room was definitely designed to make Lustris seem manly, powerful, and dangerous. It was working.

"There in the corner!" Garrett pointed.

On a pedestal in the corner of the room was the book. It was still open, and the pages continued to turn endlessly and gave off a golden light.

"Grab it and go," Garrett instructed.

David quickly walked over to the book, handled it with care, and showed it to Garrett.

"Great, let's get out of here!" Garrett said.

David noticed light on Garrett's face as he motioned for him and David to leave. It was coming from a different direction than the book in David's hand.

"What is it?" Garrett asked, confused.

"Light," David answered and jerked his head toward the window.

"It couldn't be dawn already," Garrett guessed, as they went closer to investigate.

Below, the entire barn was in flames.

Chapter Eighteen

The boys ran as quickly as they could to the barn.

"Where do we start?" David yelled.

"I don't know!" Garrett yelled back.

They circled the perimeter and found hands struggling at an open window where smoke was pouring out. Close by, a female screamed.

"Gretchen!" Garrett yelled.

"Garrett!" Gretchen was just inside the burning building. "Garrett, my dress is caught. I'm stuck!"

David watched Garrett get a running start, plant his hands on the window sill, and leap into the barn. He disappeared into the smoke.

"Garrett!" David yelled.

There was no response.

David heard a ripping noise close to the window. *Is that them? Did he find her?*

Gretchen's hands at the window answered David's questions. He ran to help her out. Gretchen landed, coughing into David's arms. Garrett jumped out after her. Gretchen was struggling for air, trying to tell David something important.

Suddenly, a burning rafter came down and smashed a hole through a nearby wall.

"Hannah is still in there!" Gretchen managed to yell.

Without thinking, David sprinted to the collapsed wall and leaped inside.

The entire place was hot, and he began sweating instantly. He could hardly breathe or see through the smoke.

"Hannah!"

Her voice called back to him from above. "David!"

There was another voice, too. "I'll kill you!" David had to help her.

David fumbled around trying to locate the way up. Eventually, he found the ladder and climbed above the flames. The ladder was smoldering and it burned his hands, but he made it to the top. Hannah was pressed against a wall. Lustris staggered before her with his dagger. He lunged toward her, but she ran to the side and his blade pierced the wall instead. Hannah ran into David's embrace. They turned back to the ladder, but it crumbled into red embers before their eyes. David started to back up. His feet met the edge of the hay loft, and he looked down at the flames of the barn floor below.

Lustris unstuck his blade and turned toward David and Hannah. He was crazed. He snarled as he ran in their direction, his blade eager to stick into some flesh. David held Hannah tight against him. At the last possible moment, he threw Hannah to the side. Lustris stumbled between them. With a huge push, David helped him continue off of the loft and toward the floor. Lustris landed in a crumpled heap. The last thing he must have seen was the burning roof collapsing on top of him.

"David!" Hannah yelled. "How do we get out of here?"

"We'll find a way," he promised. He helped her up and held her close again. They made their way toward the back of the barn. David managed to find a door on the loft level that offered a way out. He looked out into the darkness and found a pile of hay that had not yet caught fire.

"We have to jump!"

"Are you crazy?" Hannah protested.

"It's jump or burn!"

"You win!"

They held each other's hands tightly and jumped at the same time down into the hay.

Chapter Nineteen

It was a risky stunt, but they did what they had to do in order to get Mr. Linden's book back safely. Per Gretchen's suggestion, David carried it in a wooden crate back to the house. She thought that a magical book that turns its own illuminated golden pages and transports people to different worlds might catch some attention. Some golden light did creep out of the crate's cracks, but the pedestrians at this hour were hardly awake enough to notice.

When they got to Gretchen's house, David decided, "We'll just go inside, get out the book, and make our way home." He turned to enter the house, but he was struck surprisingly hard in the stomach.

Did this crate in my hands just attack me?

He looked down, confused by the black and silver arrow sticking out of the front of the crate. Before David could figure anything out, another arrow landed in Gretchen's front door.

"Again? You have got to be kidding me!" David yelled.

The four of them scrambled around the corner of Gretchen's house to escape the assault.

"This way," Garrett instructed.

He led them around back to where he had tied the two horses. David and Garrett climbed up, and Hannah and Gretchen sat behind them. Hannah held the crate.

"If we move quickly, we can lose them in the forest," Garrett suggested.

David stuck his heels into the horse's side and raced off in the direction of the forest.

They stopped the horses when Garrett was sure that they had lost whoever it was with the arrows. Everyone dismounted. David took the crate from Hannah and threw it angrily onto the ground.

"What the heck is going on now?"

"This is what I told you would happen. It's not safe to be you, David," Gretchen replied. "Especially now that everyone knows you are absolutely next in line to be Morgana's husband."

"But no one could have known," Hannah pointed out. "Morgana emptied the room before she made her proposal. It was just me, David, Morgana—"

"And Lord Valstayne," David finished.

Garrett went to the crate and pulled out the black and silver arrow. "This is no ordinary arrow," he said. "Look at its markings."

"Who would label their murder weapon?" David wondered.

"It looks like a crest painted there on the shaft," Hannah remarked. "Seems like an odd thing to do."

"This means," Garrett explained, "that you now have a hired army after you, not just some lonely assassin." He looked closer at the arrow. "Gretchen, come look at this. Tell me what you see here."

She studied it and then sighed with concern. "A red boar's head."

"That's what I was afraid of. It sort of all makes sense now."

"What is it?" Hannah asked.

"You're sure that it was only you, David, Morgana, and Valstayne who knew what was going on?" Garrett questioned.

"We were the only people left in the Great Hall," Hannah verified. "Why?"

"You think Lord Valstayne is responsible for this," David answered.

Garrett threw down the arrow. "That is his family's crest. Lord Valstayne ordered this attack."

"But why would he do that?" Gretchen asked.

"Simple," Garrett replied. "As chief advisor, he has the most to lose if Morgana marries. He doesn't want to give up his power. If Morgana marries, her husband will rule, and he loses almost everything. To make sure he stays on top, he's been ordering hits on all her future husbands."

"What are we going to do?" Hannah asked.

"You and David are going home."

David agreed. "The only way to end all this is to find the missing heirs and bring them back to Ethelrod as soon as possible. Then it's over. We'll do what we can here."

"Time to go then!" Hannah said.

David shook hands with the honorable Sir Garrett of the Castle Guard and hugged his dear friend, Gretchen, with a tight squeeze. David and Hannah stood side by side in the woods across from Gretchen and Garrett. David opened the crate and held the book out in front of him.

He looked at Hannah. "Here we go."

David pushed on the soft red leather in an attempt to close the golden pages of the book. He knew it would take a lot of force. He continued to push with all of his strength. As the covers got closer and closer together, the light got brighter and brighter until David had to clamp his eyes shut for fear of becoming blind.

When David opened his eyes, he had to adjust them to the light in the room around him. They were back in Mr. Linden's library. He looked down at the book in his hands that now only seemed to be a regular, old ordinary book.

He turned to his side and announced, "Hannah, we made it!" But all he found was a chair. He turned the other way. Tables.

"Hannah?"

With his head like a swivel, he started spinning around trying to catch a glimpse of her. He was breathing fast.

"Hannah?" Nothing. "Hannah!"

A pair of strong arms stopped David abruptly.

"David…" It was Mr. Linden. "David, where is my daughter? Did she come back with you?"

David tried pushing him away in order to keep looking for her.

"David, where is Hannah?"

David could only shake his head, still distracted.

"David! David you have to listen to me carefully." Mr. Linden's hands held his face still. "David, were you and Hannah touching when you closed the book?"

"No," David replied softly.

Mr. Linden collapsed into a nearby chair, and David realized with dread that he had returned without her. Hannah was still in Ethelrod.

"Okay, okay, okay. If the book lets us return, then we can get her back. Quick, tell me everything that happened while you were away."

David didn't like Mr. Linden's use of the word "if." *He had said "if" the book lets us return. Was there a chance it wouldn't?* David fought back the building urge to let loose his hot tears and struggled to tell Mr. Linden everything. He told Mr. Linden about Garrett and Gretchen, about Lustris and Balthazar, about Queen Morgana and Lord Valstayne, and finished with Riordan's plan of returning the missing heirs to restore order and peace.

Mr. Linden stayed quiet.

"Mr. Linden," David started. "Before, you told me the book only worked if it had what it needed."

"Yes," Mr. Linden replied.

"And you are the visitor from long ago, are you not?"

"I am, but David!"

"Well, that's it! You can find the missing heirs."

"David, about the heirs?"

David was on a roll. "We can make an exchange, use them to enter Ethelrod so we can bring Hannah back. They can stay and everything will be all right. Then, we can all come home again the way it ought to be."

"David!" Mr. Linden yelled to get his attention.

"What is it?"

"About the heirs…"

"Yes?"

"David, the missing heirs to Ethelrod's throne…they're your parents."

Chapter Twenty

It felt like forever since he'd been home instead of just a few summer months. In the passenger seat, David sat and stared at his modest home. He didn't feel like the same person who had left. So much had happened, and there was still so much to put right.

"Want me to go in with you?" Mr. Linden asked.

"I think I got this."

David exited the car and traversed the walkway that led to his front porch. At first, a sense of comfort came over him. There was an unusual silence.

Maybe the couples' retreat worked.

A few steps later that thought was crushed. His parents' fights could not be contained by walls.

"But George, think about all of the possibilities a great education can offer an individual." David knew his mother, Elizabeth, was always looking to the future. "Think about our son! Think of everything he could do and become with a college degree."

David decided to stay on the porch and listen.

"He would be just as fine back home as he is here," George argued.

"Really?" Elizabeth questioned critically. "You honestly believe his future would be as bright as it could be here?"

David was used to his parents' arguments being about him, but after this summer's events, the context made more sense. *Back home?* David always thought they meant his childhood home before this one. Boy, was he wrong. *They mean Ethelrod.*

"Times have changed. He could be fine."

"I don't believe it."

"Elizabeth—" George started.

"No!" she interrupted. "I saw him looking at medical schools. I read his college application essays about his dream to become a doctor. Leaving here smashes any chance he has of that, and you know it. Even if he changes his mind to law or business, it doesn't matter. It's over if we leave."

David tried to remember any of the jobs he came across while he was in Ethelrod. *King, queen, merchant, fisherman, blacksmith, historian, horrible sheriff, blood-thirsty royal advisor.* Nope. None of those honestly seemed appealing to him.

"So it seems that once again our kid is the deciding factor. I would love to get his opinion on this, but no. You had to send him away!"

Did my parents send me away so they could talk about Ethelrod without me?

All of their old fights over the past year were starting to become clearer now that he knew about his parents' secret past.

"You want him living here like this? Seeing his parents constantly arguing? George, I love you. I do. But how we are living, who we are becoming, is not what I want our son to see."

"Which is why we need to go back. Think of David."

"I am," she answered.

Mr. Linden cleared his throat right behind David standing on the porch. David was so surprised, he jumped. "Gosh," he whispered.

Mr. Linden put his hand on David's shoulder. "Don't you think we should go inside?" Mr. Linden whispered in return. David noticed he had brought the red book and David's sword. Even more useful was Mr. Linden's supportive smile.

David nodded. He took a deep breath to gather his strength and resolve. He raised his arm and rapped sharply three times on the front door.

The shouting died down, and the sound of footsteps came to the front door. When the couple opened it and stared at their visitors on the porch, David could see the shock on their faces.

"David?" Elizabeth stumbled.

"Hi, Mom!"

"Tom?" George gaped.

"Hello, George," replied Mr. Linden. "David knows about Ethelrod."

"We sent him to you so he could escape all this Ethelrod talk!" George bellowed.

"And you're saying he knows everything?" Elizabeth asked. "About us and who we are? You had no right! That was our secret to share when we were ready."

"I had no choice, Elizabeth," Mr. Linden explained. "It's not like I blurted out a secret. He's been there! He knows now…about you, about Ethelrod, about the book—"

"I can't believe you brought that *thing* inside my house," she screamed. "And why on earth does David have a sword?"

"We sent him to you to take care of him," George yelled, "not to send him into battle! This was not a choice for you to make."

"It was hardly a choice." This was the first time David had spoken since he and Mr. Linden started telling his parents the story. David always imagined that he was the one who was in control of the travelling, as Mr. Linden seemed to be when he worked the book. Now, it looked like the book itself was doing all the work and making the decisions.

"And it's not a choice now," David continued. "We have to go back, and you have to come with us. It won't work without you."

"Right," Elizabeth said, "because we are the only ones who can save the kingdom. There isn't anyone else?"

"Elizabeth," George pleaded, "it looks like it is our responsibility to go back."

"Don't talk to me about responsibility! The only reason you want to go back is because you miss all the glory and attention."

"And why not?" George interjected. "I was a prince! Much better than who I am here. There I'd be a king. And so would David eventually. Can't you see it'd be better for us? You are so selfish sometimes!"

"Selfish?!" Elizabeth yelled. "It's selfish for me to want the best life available for my son? To look out for a person I love? He is going to be a doctor."

"Hey," David interrupted. "I thought we talked about my privacy."

"It was only to proofread before we mailed them off," Elizabeth eased. "They were very well written. The point is, David, that you would not have that possibility anymore if we left."

"It's not just about us anymore," David said. "It's more than that." He looked at Mr. Linden.

"Right, it's the entire country now," George added.

"And Hannah," came a whisper from the corner of the room. It was Mr. Linden. The Wilsons stopped and stared at him.

"Who?" Elizabeth asked.

"Hannah," David answered.

"Who's Hannah?" George wondered.

"My daughter," Mr. Linden explained. "Please, Elizabeth."

"I'm going to forget the fact that you have a daughter you never told us about, Tom," she replied. "It seems like there is no choice, but we have to talk about this more. I'm still not sure returning is the best for our family. We need time."

"We don't have time," David interceded. "Time moves faster in Ethelrod than it does here. A week here is a year in Ethelrod! We can't wait forever before we decide to bring Hannah back."

"A week is a year?" George sounded surprised. "Well, think about it, Elizabeth. David was born here and look how old he is now. We were almost eighteen when we left with Tom. There are fifty-two weeks in a year, and we've been gone almost twenty! Surely there has been enough advancement in our time gone to convince you to return."

"Actually, George," Mr. Linden said, "I'm sorry but the way David talks about it, it seems Ethelrod is exactly the same."

"How can that be?" Elizabeth asked.

"Even though centuries have passed since you lived there, it seems like the world of Ethelrod remains stagnant. Only the people and the rulers have changed. And it does not seem to be for the better." Mr. Linden wanted to get his daughter back, but David appreciated that he was not going to lie to his friend to get what he so desperately wanted.

"We have to go back, Lizzie," George reasoned.

"Don't pretend that you aren't primarily thinking of yourself," Elizabeth replied.

"Even if I am," George gave in, "are you going to let a little girl take our place?"

"I'm sorry." Elizabeth began to cry. "I can't go back."

David's parents started yelling again. First George, then Elizabeth. Mr. Linden attempted to referee, trying to calm one down and then the other. David knew it was hopeless. He covered his ears to keep out the shouting and placed his head between his knees.

What am I going to do? If only there were a way to fix this.

He understood both sides of his parents' argument, but David could only think of Hannah. It had already been a few days. He was worried about her. It made him sick to think of anything horrible happening to her. He missed her terribly. If only his parents could have this fight in Ethelrod and save everybody some time. If they just got a taste of their former home, maybe they would be able to decide. Here, it was hopeless. David had to get everyone out of this mess, but how?

A quick, warm breeze brushed the hair on his forehead. It wasn't particularly a hot day, so David looked outside to check the weather. It was nice, but the breeze was warm. David didn't understand. He checked the other windows of the room. All of the windows were shut. Had he imagined the breeze? David touched his forehead in confusion. Then, he looked down at the table.

Somewhere during the discussion, if it could be called that, Mr. Linden had set the book down on the table. It was open.

Are the pages glowing?

"Guys?" David called.

They weren't listening. They couldn't hear him over their own yelling.

"Guys!" No response from the adults.

David knelt on the floor in front of the coffee table, watching the book intently. David felt another breeze and a strong pressure knock into his side. It hurt. He stood up in amazement. His parents and Mr. Linden did not notice it yet. Another blow to the leg and David almost fell over. He wondered why it was only affecting him until—

"Ow!" his mother yelled. She was talking to Mr. Linden, but turned to accuse her husband. "Did you just push me?" There was an armchair in between them so it couldn't have been George. "Oh, no…" She noticed the open book. "David? What did you do?"

"It wasn't me," he tried to explain.

"It was the book," Mr. Linden yelled above the now-roaring wind. "Come on, everyone, hold on!" Mr. Linden motioned for everyone to move toward the book.

"No! I won't go!" She started to walk away, pushing the whipping hair out of her face. George grabbed her hand and she stopped.

"I can't do this without you, love," he said.

Elizabeth bent a little at the knees and folded herself into him, almost collapsing, hiding her face between George's shoulder and neck. He guided her to the coffee table where Mr. Linden and David were already waiting.

The wind was still roaring. The forceful blows hadn't stopped either. David thought this must be what being inside a tornado would be like if invisible giant fists were also beating him up at the same time. The furniture around them bumped across the room, and the four of them huddled closer. The cardboard pieces of Elizabeth's almost-completed puzzle flew around the room, stinging when they hit David's bare skin. David's beloved lumpy couch crashed against the far wall. Then he remembered. *The sword!* He knew he needed to get it back. He tried to break from the pack, but Mr. Linden caught him again.

"No, David!" he called.

"I have to get the sword!" David yelled back over the noise.

Mr. Linden's grip lessened, but it was still not enough for David to get at the sword. He clawed at the carpet to reach the sword glinting at him. He was almost there. He could feel the floor begin to vibrate. The vibrating got more intense. Along with the wind blowing, it felt and sounded like a stampede was coming their way. David reached for the sword again and missed.

"David, come back!" his mom called.

The force of the wind and the blows, the sound of the roaring, and the shaking floor mixed now with what sounded like the grunting and neighing of animals and the clang of metal; it was all too much. The feeling of pressure was too much. David felt himself black out. He summoned all of his strength and made one final reach. He grasped the handle of the sword, but in doing so Mr. Linden lost his grip. David fell to the ground, his face landing in the dirt.

Dirt?

It didn't matter if Mr. Linden had let go. All four of them were back in Ethelrod.

Chapter Twenty-one

David didn't have enough time to be excited. They had landed in the middle of a battle. David quickly stood up to take in the scene. Men on horses and on foot were fighting on a large path in the middle of the woods of Ethelrod. It was chaos. David was stunned. A blow crashed into David's shoulder blade as a horse raced past him. David was knocked to the ground and scrambled backward to the edge of the trail to avoid being trampled by the other horses that followed. The men in armor were definitely in hot pursuit of something or someone.

Where are my parents? Where is Mr. Linden?

A voice from behind him answered his thoughts. "David," it whispered above the noise of the horses and men. David turned around but could not find anyone. "David!" Then he saw them, three pairs of eyes staring at him through the fern undergrowth at the side of the trail. David ran over and joined them, keeping low.

From their hiding spot, they waited until all signs of the fight were gone before standing up and addressing the situation.

"Well, we're definitely back," George said. He looked at his wife. "Elizabeth, are you okay?"

"I'm fine," she answered.

George stared at her. "You sure?"

"We're here now," Elizabeth reasoned. "And I know the book won't let any of us return until it means for us to, so let's just go."

"But where to?" Tom asked. All three of them looked to David.

He was going to have to make a decision. The biggest battle had been getting his parents to come back to Ethelrod. Now that he had, David realized he hadn't thought too much further in advance.

"Well," he started, "we—"

But David was interrupted by crashing sounds nearby. Leaves rustled and twigs broke. Whoever, or whatever, was coming through the forest was getting closer. Another decision. *What to do?* David gripped the sword in his hand. "Get behind me," he commanded, as he raised the sword in the direction of the sounds, which were almost on top of them now.

David adjusted his grip on the sword just as a figure in armor broke through to the clearing. The figure saw David's sword and instantly raised its hands. Everyone stood still. The figure started to lower its hands slowly.

"Don't move!" David shouted.

One of the figure's hands moved toward David to show it meant no harm, but the other continued toward the helmet.

"I'm warning you," David continued, taking a few steps forward.

The figure removed its helmet to reveal a young man with dark blond hair. "David?"

David recognized him at once. He ran to the man and gave him a hug. It was Garrett.

"David, who is this?" his mother asked.

"Mom, Dad, Mr. Linden, this is Sir Garrett of the Castle Guard."

"Pleased to meet you," Garrett smiled.

"Castle Guard. Very impressive!" George stated. Garrett nodded in appreciation.

"And I'm a captain now, David. Got a promotion. Youngest in our history."

"Garrett, what's going on here?" David asked.

"The Castle Guard is attempting to round up some rebels," he answered.

"Rebels?" Elizabeth questioned.

"Yes, ma'am. The rumor has been spreading that Queen Morgana is not the rightful queen and that she should step down. Lord Valstayne, her advisor who wishes to see her remain in power, has the Castle Guard trying to round them up and quiet them."

"And you're helping them? Leading them even?" David asked confusedly. "How could you?"

"Relax," Garrett replied. "The Castle Guard didn't catch any rebels in this raid."

"How is that possible?" George asked.

"Quite easily when the rebels have someone inside the Castle Guard to give them warning." Garrett winked.

David understood. "I'm sorry, Garrett. That's brilliant! So you've been working to spread the news all this time?"

"I have, but Riordan has been helping to do most of the more difficult convincing."

"Riordan?" Elizabeth asked.

"The High Historian and Keeper of Records," David answered. "And how about Gretchen, where is she?"

"Believe it or not," Garrett explained, "she has landed a position as a lady-in-waiting to the queen herself. She's gathering what information she can and even trying to plant seeds of doubt in Morgana. She was able to gain the queen's trust quite early, and I believe she has been making some real progress. We don't get to see each other much, what with starting an uprising and all."

"This is all great," Mr. Linden interrupted, surprising everyone. "But what about my daughter?"

"Oh, right!" David felt a little ashamed that he had let the excitement of returning get him off track of finding his friend. "Garrett, how long have I been gone?"

"Six months this time," he replied.

"Oh, my," said Mr. Linden. "Hannah's been here alone for six months."

"Who is this?" Garrett asked.

"Hannah's dad, Mr. Tom Linden," David answered. "We came to get her and bring her home. Where is she?"

"Things got a little complicated after you left," Garrett explained. "After Lustris's body was found in the wreckage of the barn, an investigation led straight to Hannah's involvement, partly because she was a stranger with no background, but mainly because that old apple seller pointed a finger. However, they also think she can be used to find you, David."

"Find me?"

"You didn't think Queen Morgana would let you get away that easily after you agreed to marry her and everything."

"Oh, I totally forgot about the engagement."

"Engagement!" his mother squealed. "What?"

"It's a long story, but Morgana can't still expect that to go on, can she?"

"Queen Morgana has forbidden all marriages until your return. If she can't get married, no one can. She may be open to the idea of giving up her throne, since it has only caused her heartache and trouble, but she is definitely not ready to give you up, her new chance at happiness."

"Perfect."

"We've had to hide Hannah. There's a reward for her and everything. Hannah is seeking sanctuary, unknown to the authorities, with a religious group of women on the outskirts of the Southern Plains. We put her there until you came back, and it was safe again."

"Do you mean the Ladies of the Veil? Are they still in existence?" Mr. Linden questioned.

"I do, and they are."

"I must go at once."

Mr. Linden started to leave, but George caught his arm and stopped him. "Hold on, Tom. We need to think about this first. We can't just go running around Ethelrod the minute we get here."

"Hannah's been alone here for six months," Mr. Linden pleaded.

"We need to stick together," Elizabeth reasoned. "We're in this as a team now." She looked to George. "For better or for worse."

"The safest way for Hannah to return is if her name is cleared," Garrett suggested. "The only real way to do that is to remove Lord Valstayne or Queen Morgana or both. But we can only do that with the heirs of old. Only they can come back and take the throne. David, it was your job to go and find them and bring them back. Where are they?"

"Garrett," David began, "I would like you to meet my parents."

Chapter Twenty-two

"The best thing is to present them at court to reclaim the throne," Garrett explained. "This announcement should gather enough people to our side and to oust Morgana. There is already enough doubt and wonder, even within the courtiers, that surely a presentation of the heirs by David the Champion himself would be hard to dispute."

"That sounds great, but you don't need me. I've got to go get Hannah. Now," Mr. Linden said, as he mounted Garrett's second horse. Along with his glowing book, he rode off toward the Southern Plains to find his daughter.

David, his father, and Sir Garrett walked alongside his mother, who sat on the remaining horse. It would take longer than David was used to for them to walk from the forests of Ethelrod to the High Kingdom, but he didn't mind. He was back. For now.

"I guess I never thought about it before," David wondered.

"What's that?" Elizabeth asked.

"I've never been in Ethelrod long enough to think about the geography. I never knew there were Southern Plains before. I only know about the places I've been."

"That's understandable," replied Garrett. "Basically when you've been here, you've traveled on a straight line east and west. There's the Western Shore, the forests in the center, and the High Kingdom in the east."

"I'm assuming the Southern Plains are in the south," David joked.

"Endless grasslands as far as the eye can see," George added. "And no recordable end unless something has changed since we have been gone."

"That is still the same," Garrett said. "No one who has ever gone far enough to find the end has ever made it back. No water, no food, just continuous tall grass."

"Yikes! And how about in the north?"

"The Northern Mountains, a mountain range that is way too dangerous to pass if you get far enough into them," his mother answered.

"You two know your geography," Garrett said, amazed. "Your knowledge of Ethelrod will definitely help us when we get to court. And besides, David, the mountains are rumored to be inhabited by monsters."

"Monsters?"

"Treasure-seekers," Garrett answered.

"You know them as dragons," George explained. "They are greedy, nasty devils who are very protective of their caves, which are said to be filled with gold and treasure they have acquired over time. They can live for centuries, but no one knows for sure."

"No one has ever seen one or found one of their caves," Garrett continued. "But that doesn't stop the stories and legends from getting told before bedtime. They might even get blamed every now and then for missing objects."

"Missing objects?" David asked.

"Yes," Elizabeth said. "Treasure-seekers love to gather treasure. If something precious goes missing, it's much easier to blame a myth than admit you lost it."

"For example," Garrett said, "a treasure-seeker would love to get his hands on that sword of yours."

Oddly enough, David had grown used to walking around with a sword at his waist.

"I don't like you walking around with a deadly weapon," Elizabeth said.

David figured years away in the real world probably had that effect on people. David called it the "real world" because it was where he was born and where he had spent the majority of his life. This was not true for his parents. Sure, they had spent more than half of their lives with David, but they were born in Ethelrod. *Which one was the "real world" for them? If forced to choose, which world would they decide to call home?*

David shook the thought from his mind.

"What? This old thing?" David said, as he motioned toward the sword.

"Hey," George called, "let me see that." David took out the sword and passed it to his father. "It can't be," he whispered. "Where did you get this?"

"From my first time in Ethelrod," David answered. "It was on my bed when I arrived, and I had to use it when I was forced to fight in the tournament duel where I became champion."

"Fascinating," George whispered again.

"What is?" Elizabeth asked.

"This is my sword!" George said astonished. "It was a birthday present from my father. I had it that day we left with Tom."

Elizabeth leaned down from the horse for a closer look. "I remember it now. That was centuries ago, but here it is!"

"We left, but it stayed behind. And somehow it ended up in David's possession. I bet there is quite a story behind this sword's journey." George studied the blade in his hands.

"Quite a story indeed," Garrett agreed.

"Where's the shield?"

"The what?" David asked.

"When I left the sword behind, I also left its matching shield with the family crest. See here on the hilt? A stag. The shield has the same symbol."

"I just have the sword."

"No one's seen the shield," Garrett said. "But if the sword was yours, then this is exactly what we need to prove who you two are. We are set! We couldn't have asked for a better coincidence." Garrett was visibly excited at the prospect of a brighter future for his country under the new, upcoming regime.

"That is if we ever get there," Elizabeth said. "It seems by the time we get to the High Kingdom, Tom will already be back with Hannah. This is taking forever."

"I would have brought more horses if I had known you were coming, but David has a habit of just randomly showing up as he pleases." Garrett nudged David playfully.

"How far away is the convent or whatever?" David asked.

"The Ladies of the Veil are on the outskirts of the Southern Plains. The way Tom flew off on that horse, I expect he's travelling faster than the speed of sound," George guessed.

"I don't envy that horse," Elizabeth added. "I bet he's working it hard to get his girl back. Can you blame him?" She looked down at David. "Parents will do anything for their children. They'd travel to the ends of the earth if they had to."

"Ends of the world, huh?" David thought for a moment. "Say, what's outside of Ethelrod?"

"What?" Garrett questioned.

"Outside of Ethelrod," David repeated.

"No one knows," George replied. "You've got the coastlines on each side and the mountains and plains above and below."

"What about the sea? Surely someone has gone somewhere outside of Ethelrod."

"David, think about it," Garrett started. "How many ships have you seen in your time in Ethelrod? And I'm not talking boats like you'd see in the fishing villages of the Western Shore where Gretchen's family lives. I mean full-on ships."

David hadn't seen anything like that in Ethelrod. "None, I guess."

"And you won't either," Elizabeth explained. "Away from the shores are treacherous coral reefs that destroy and sink anything that tries to sail out too far."

"Ethelrod is isolated," George said. "So you can imagine how eager we were to leave. To listen to Tom talk about where he came from was just too much. I had to be a part of it. *We* had to be a part of it. That's why we were going with Tom, whether he wanted us to come or not."

"It seems you can't avoid your fate, though," Elizabeth added. "Our responsibility remains."

At that moment, the thick trees cleared and opened into a field with green grass and colorful wildflowers. At the edge of the field, thatched and slate roofs winked at the travelers with the sun's reflection. They grew taller and closer together as they seemed to rise up to the large stone towers of the castle jutting out of the center of the magnificent city.

"We're back," Elizabeth announced.

Did David see the glimpse of a smile at the corners of her mouth?

Chapter Twenty-three

The plan was a little shaky, but it was set.

"I've been receiving letters from Gretchen," Garrett said. "I believe that Queen Morgana might be convinced to step down now that someone with a legitimate right has finally come along after all these centuries of Morgana's family's reign as ruling stewards."

"Will the people of Ethelrod be eager to accept new rulers?" Elizabeth asked.

"Yes, if it means bringing an end to feudal wars and a reign of peace for the kingdom," Garrett answered.

"And surely Morgana would like to see an end to the 'curse' linked between her sitting on the throne and not being able to find a lasting love," David added. "However, these are a lot of assumptions."

"The sword will be a useful prop in the presentation," George said. "Hopefully our backstory will be convincing enough."

David believed it, but he had grown used to the fantastic being reality this summer. Garrett believed it, or did he just hope it? No matter what complexities lay ahead, the time for planning and thinking was over and the time for action had begun. They were now inside the outer walls of the High Kingdom.

It was easy to pass the outer walls unnoticed with Garrett ushering them in, but it grew harder to remain anonymous once they travelled farther into the heart of the city. The people were busy trading and selling or shopping and buying, but the group still received the occasional glances and glares. As they made their way deeper into the city, the whispers started, and then murmurs, and finally the audible recognitions came.

"Are these more visitors?"

"They seem to be coming all the time now."

"Doesn't that boy seem familiar?"

"Who is that with that member of the Castle Guard?"

"Is that David the Champion?"

"It is! David the Champion has returned!"

David tried to hide his face by turning in toward his mother and the horse, but it was hopeless. No doubt Morgana had the whole kingdom on the lookout for her runaway fiancé.

"But who are those others with him?"

"That man and woman, who are they?"

"Haven't you heard the rumors?"

"You don't suppose…could it really be?"

"Has David found the missing heirs?"

"It can't be them."

"It might be them."

"Don't let anyone hear you talking like that too loudly."

"It still might be them."

From what he gathered, David figured they were excited about his return. At least now all those young couples in love might be able to get married. However, the presence of his parents had a different effect. He wasn't sure how to place it. Some people seemed excited, while others hushed up and drew away as the four of them passed by. Garrett had said there had been raids on those with rebellious ideas. On the way over, he described entire towns set aflame because of rumors of organized rebellion. Those were smaller villages, but even now some of these people were probably worried about what these whispers of change might do to them if they were caught standing too near to the sedition.

Sir Garrett led David, George, and Elizabeth to the town square where the castle gate was located. He spoke to a guard inside the iron portcullis.

"Sir Garrett of the Castle Guard," he announced, "with visitors to be presented to Her Majesty Queen Morgana."

"Goodness sake, Garrett," the other guard replied, as he raised the portcullis. "We'd given you up. All of the others returned hours ago. Who have you brought with you?"

"I can't explain at the moment," Garrett replied. "We must see the queen at once."

"I assume you will find her in the throne room with all the other courtiers as usual."

"Thanks, Andrew." Garrett shook the guard's hand and led the others inside, as the portcullis was lowered again.

The walls surrounding the castle circumscribed the towers and the grounds. To enter into the main courtyard, one had to travel the curving stone-walled path before being allowed inside. It was a tedious walk if you had to make it every day, but it was very useful for protection. David looked up and watched the members of the Castle Guard looking down on them from both sides or as they crossed the various connections between the platforms overhead.

Eventually they made it into the fine courtyard where George helped Elizabeth off the horse, which was then led toward the stables per Sir Garrett's request.

"Are we ready?" Garrett asked.

"It's now or never," George said. He held out his hand for Elizabeth. She took his hand firmly. "Here we go!"

It had only been a week for David since he had been inside that room, but it was still impressive. George and Elizabeth looked around with a hint of excitement, yet David noticed it was more out of remembrance than novelty.

At the far end was a vibrant rose window of colored glass. Underneath was a platform where an odd-looking woman sat in an elaborate chair, talking to a man who stood next to her. David had to stand on his toes to look over the crowd of people, but he knew it was Queen Morgana. She had let herself go even more during the last six months, if that was even possible. She had looked somewhat disheveled on his last visit, but now she was slightly more ragged with an ill-fitting gown that seemed to swallow her. Crazy hair stuck out in all directions from whatever style she had originally chosen. She looked thinner and paler, too. David felt a twinge of sorrow for her. Her life hadn't started out this way. She hadn't caused these wars on purpose. David wasn't sure he would have made any better decisions in her shoes. However, this didn't change the fact that David's goal remained to replace her with his parents if she would let him. He took a deep breath.

As they made their way through the finely dressed courtiers, David for the first time noticed how completely underdressed he was. He was still wearing his jeans and a T-shirt. He must have looked truly bizarre because the faces were at first snooty and disgusted before they turned to recognition. They would know David the Champion anywhere. David saw a young boy walking quickly along one of the walls, past them, and up toward where the queen was positioned. He knelt in front of her and whispered an announcement that David could not hear. He could easily guess its contents, though, when she sat upright and started scanning the room. She knew he was here.

When they broke free from the crowd and into the opening in front of Queen Morgana, she locked eyes with David and an eerie smile grew across her face. The man next to her did not smile. His scowl remained. David met this man's stare. It was Lord Valstayne, still dangerous and venomous as ever, especially when it came to David. Could it be possible that he was even more evil looking?

"My queen! May I present—" Sir Garrett started to announce,

but he was interrupted by Morgana.

"Sir Garrett, this is the second time you have brought me David the Champion. Once on request and now by your own will you return him. Your loyalty is to be rewarded."

Garrett nodded and stepped back, quickly glancing to his left. David followed his glance to a row of women he hadn't noticed yet. They were lined up near Queen Morgana and wore dresses of the same pale blue. He studied the faces until he found her. There, trying to hide an obvious smile and making a waving motion with her hand at her waist, was Gretchen. David nodded briefly before turning back to the queen.

"And David," Morgana fake pouted. "What happened, dearest? We were all set to be married and you left. If I didn't know about your constant appearing and disappearing, I might have taken it personally." She scooted over in her throne and patted some free space for David to come join her. He felt very uncomfortable with this older, crazy woman flirting with him.

This was a dangerous situation, and David had to think carefully before he spoke.

Maybe I just get straight to the point about my parents?

Seeing Lord Valstayne again made his blood boil as he remembered the failed assassination attempt.

Should I point the finger at Lord Valstayne for making me leave so quickly?

Surely, the queen would not like that. But Valstayne was deadly. This was very delicate indeed.

"Your Majesty," he began, "how kind of you to remember my unfortunate condition. You are quite right in thinking that I had no choice but to leave." David shifted his eyes to Valstayne for a moment, which the queen's advisor caught. "However, I have returned and brought my parents to bear joyous witness to whatever celebrations are in Ethelrod's future." George bowed and Elizabeth curtseyed.

Morgana gave a sigh of relief and patted the spot next to her again. David had no choice but to join her. The space was cramped. He was stuck between the armrest and the copious amount of stiff fabric from the queen's dress.

"You brought your family!" Morgana said excitedly. "How nice of them to join us."

David looked at his parents, then at Garrett, Gretchen, and the courtiers. Finally, David watched Valstayne standing next to Queen Morgana. David knew it was risky, but it had to be done.

"My queen," he said, "I would be happy to introduce you to my parents, but I must ask you a question. I will gladly share my future with you, but I would like to know more about your family history if I am going to be a part of it. Since I have been back," he gulped, "I have heard rumors."

Morgana nervously smiled at David, but she never lost her stately composure. She waved to the rest of the crowd in the room and said sweetly, "Back to what you were doing."

The courtiers in the room seemed to obey. They all returned to their conversations and milling about as they had been before David arrived. Yet, David did notice one man with a feather in his hat simply mouthing fake words as he kept his eyes in their direction. Members of the crowd were still very interested in listening in on the private conversation happening in front of them.

Morgana gave David the same fake smile. "Dearest, what have you heard?" she asked.

"Only that there may be others with claims to the throne," he replied. "I wouldn't want to marry into an uprising. You understand."

"Oh, of course," Morgana agreed. "And it is very wise of David the Champion to be thinking of such survival scenarios." She patted him on the knee. "But there is no need to be worried, my love. Those rumors are simply not true!"

"Not true?"

"Of course not. My family has ruled Ethelrod for centuries. If it were true, this stewardship would be known to me. And besides, I've just had a brilliant idea from one of my ladies-in-waiting, Gretchen. Wonderful girl. I believe you know her, do you not? Gretchen, come here." Gretchen curtseyed and left her spot in line. "Gretchen, I would like my fan." Gretchen nodded and went to a table.

"Gretchen has come up with a way to prove my legitimacy."

"Has she?"

"Yes, she recommended that I use some castle resources to my benefit. To prove my claim, I have decided to call upon the High Historian and Keeper of Records." Gretchen returned and handed a blue and silver fan to Morgana.

"Riordan," David said.

"How do you know this?" Morgana asked, surprised.

Gretchen gave David an anxious look that was unseen by the queen as she quickly returned to her spot in line.

"Oh, one hears things," David lied.

"One hears lots of things, I'm afraid, which is why Riordan has become of the utmost importance. He should be here soon actually."

"And what if," David asked carefully, "what if he proves something contrary to your beliefs?"

"Then by all means, find me my replacements!" Morgana giggled as she cracked herself up. "It would be nice to get a vacation. But honestly, David, centuries of beliefs cannot be wrong. I *am* queen."

The tall entrance doors to the Great Hall groaned open, and Morgana turned to see who had arrived. The rest of the room stopped pretending they weren't listening and copied the queen's actions. It was Riordan. The old, blind, bald man limped toward the platform. He was being walked and supported by a young man at one arm. Underneath his other arm was a large stack of yellow papers, part of a collection that David knew filled rooms beneath the castle from floor to ceiling. A path formed in the crowd as Riordan stepped forward.

"Ah, Historian," Morgana addressed him. "What have you found for me?"

"My queen." Riordan tried to bow, but stumbled on his legs. He quickly corrected himself, but he did not make the attempt again. "My assistant and I have been searching my records for you, and I have found the truth should you wish to hear it."

"Should I wish to hear it?" Morgana scoffed. "Why do you think I sent you on this fact-finding mission in the first place? Please present the records of my rightful claim to the throne."

"That's just it, Your Majesty." The room grew uncomfortably silent. Riordan shifted. "You don't have one." He said it quickly and quietly, but it did not go missed.

Morgana stood up and took a few steps forward. David took the chance to escape from his seated position and rub the large dent on his side that he was sure was permanent after being scrunched against the armrest. He tried to walk it off as he made his way back to his parents.

"Excuse me?!" she bellowed in anger. "What do you mean?"

"My assistant has found the records for me," Riordan began, motioning to the pile of old papers in his hands, "that indicate your family line started as a line of stewards positioned as rulers until the time when the rightful heirs to the kingdom were restored. This was centuries ago, your highness, which would be why the history of our people has been forgotten until now."

"Unbelievable!" Morgana turned to her ladies-in-waiting and made her way swiftly to them. "Gretchen! You told me this would ensure my position. That this would make everything better."

"Forgive me, your highness," Gretchen bent at the knees, but did not look up. She talked to the hem of Morgana's skirt instead. "But I believe I told you this method would find out the truth. Isn't that what remains important? Isn't this what you wanted in the end?"

Morgana's face went blank. She started muttering and whispering to herself. "I've been tricked."

For some reason beyond his understanding, David stepped forward to comfort her. Morgana used his arm to steady herself, but she did not look him in the eyes. Only David could hear what she was saying.

"Everything I have believed was a lie. Everything I fought so hard for. And why am I fighting so hard for something that does not even belong to me? Why have I lost so much for it? What's the point? Is this a blessing in disguise? Could this be my chance to finally break free from a life I'm now beginning to realize I never wanted?"

She met David's gaze.

"Morgana?"

She whispered back, "This is not time to think of this yet. The throne is still mine. I have a job to do. As long as it still remains my duty, I will stand strong."

David admired the sentiment but didn't understand. "I don't—"

"Trust me, David."

Morgana returned to her throne and sat down. "Well, Lord Valstayne, it would appear that the rumors are true. I sit in a throne reserved for someone else." She addressed the rest of the crowd now. "But until he or she with the rightful claim to the throne arrives, I will continue to rule as I have done."

The crowd remained silent. Morgana accepted the news somewhat graciously and professionally. That must have taken quite some work on Gretchen's side over the last months to pull off changing the queen's mind.

This was only phase one. David looked at his parents. This was their home and that was their throne, but they seemed to be looking at him to make the next decision. It was up to David to finish what he started. He would make the next move.

Chapter Twenty-four

He was about to start phase two when he heard someone scream, "David!"

Before he could turn around and say, "Now what?" two hands pressed against the sides of his face, as another face swooped toward his and pressed its warm lips against his. David didn't fight it. It felt nice. When it was finished, David stepped back as the face came into view.

"Hannah!"

Hannah had just kissed him. It's true that David had started to have feelings for Hannah at that time when they kept alternating saving each other's lives. But here she was kissing him! Obviously, she had feelings for him, too. Then, David remembered. Hannah had had six months to allow her feelings for David to grow. This was fine by him. Very naturally, David leaned in and they kissed again.

"David?" He snapped out of his momentary trance. "What's this?" Morgana asked, shocked. "Who is this?"

It was not David who answered the queen's question, but Lord Valstayne.

"Hannah, at last!" He called to the guards. "Seize her!"

The guards ripped Hannah out of David's arms and started to take her away.

"Wait," another voice called. "What's going on here?" Mr. Linden came into view, trying to take in the scene.

"Tom, what are you doing here?" George asked urgently. Softly he added, "And where is the book?"

"It's safe and hidden. Hannah was supposed to stay hidden as well," he explained. "She wanted to be of some help. She wouldn't take 'no' for an answer. Now, it's all ruined."

"Wait!" David called frantically. He turned to Morgana. "You can't. Please!"

Valstayne stepped in. "Hannah has been six months on the run, wanted for the murder of Sheriff Lustris, Your Majesty. There is nothing we can do. She must be turned over to the authorities."

"It wasn't her fault!" David looked pleadingly to Morgana for help. Morgana returned a helpless and apologetic gaze to him.

"David," she said, "if it were in my power, I would do all that I could." She looked warily at her advisor. "But this is the law. I must think of my people. Recent events being what they are, I cannot invite chaos when I am already sitting in a position where I am desperately attempting to keep a precious balance. There is nothing I can do."

David was frustrated and angry, and he couldn't help what he said next. "Then we need the rightful rulers who can!" Morgana's head jerked back as if she had been dealt a great and surprising blow. "I apologize, Your Majesty, but Ethelrod needs rulers who are not afraid to make the right choices."

"And who would that be, boy?" Morgana asked, stinging back by emphasizing David's youth.

"I would like to reintroduce my parents, George and Elizabeth Wilson."

George held out his arm, which Elizabeth took, and escorted his wife closer to the throne. They looked the part, very formal and proper. Too bad they were still wearing jeans. "I understand the recent news is quite astounding and unbelievable," George said, "but it is true."

Riordan spoke up. "David set out to find the descendants of

the missing prince and princess. You found that your parents are those heirs' descendants?"

"Not exactly," David explained.

"We are the actual missing prince and princess who long ago left this world for another, where time moves much more slowly," George replied. "We have returned to claim what is ours and restore peace to our beloved country."

"Surely, my queen," Valstayne said, hissing his "s" sounds, "this must be a desperate attempt by David to take advantage of the situation and place his own family in a place of leadership so that he too may control the throne at a later point."

"It would explain David's abilities if he came from such a lineage," Morgana reasoned.

Was she beginning to see the light? Was there a possibility this whole thing might work out for the best?

"If it would please Your Majesty," Elizabeth began, "we have brought something with us that might help put your mind at ease."

George motioned to David, who unsheathed his sword.

"We present this sword," George announced. "This is the sword I received on my eighteenth birthday when I was not much older than my son here. You will notice the stag on the handle. It is the mark of my family house. The ruling family house."

"No one can prove what you say is true," Valstayne spat. "This is a family of liars. There isn't a shred of proof to this story, and there is not a man alive who can verify what you say."

"I can." Riordan stepped forward once again. He handed the papers to the man at his arm and whispered to him. The man shuffled through the yellowed parchment and brought out a specific page that just so happened to have a picture of a sword and a shield on it.

"This record," Riordan explained, "shows the transition of two items within the castle treasury. This sword and this shield with the markings of the royal house, the symbol of a stag, were given to the prince and heir on his eighteenth birthday as both a birthday present and a pre-wedding gift by his parents. The sword and shield of Faraman have been in the family's possession for ages."

George gently squeezed Elizabeth's hand lovingly in remembrance.

David leaned over and whispered to his father, "Faraman? Who is he?"

"Not he. They. The Faramans, that's my side. Faraman means 'family.' It's my real family name until I had it legally changed for documentation back home," George whispered back.

"So my name isn't really David Wilson?"

"Of course it is. Legally, that is your name. Here, you just happen to also be a Faraman. Pretty impressive, if I say so myself."

Riordan's man finished reading the written record that told the origin of David's sword. The sword was even taken to compare its markings to those on the records. The story appeared to be true. This even seemed to be enough for Morgana.

"Well," she began, "if it is as Riordan says—"

David watched as Lord Valstayne saw his power leaving as Morgana's conviction waned, the power he had spent years accumulating at the right hand of a queen he was used to controlling quite easily until now. Lose that? Never.

"This is ridiculous!" he yelled. "The only reason any of them have this sword in the first place is because it was presented to David on the day of his contest. No more, no less. Their possession of this sword proves nothing."

Morgana was forced to agree.

David looked at Hannah, helpless in the arms of the guards, her life in danger if put on trial for murder. He looked at Gretchen and Garrett, who had spent so much time and effort on this cause that was now unraveling. Sir Garrett, who had helped David so many times, was unable to marry the girl of his dreams according to his update when David arrived.

What else had he said?

David was sure there was some other possibility as he tried to remember this day's previous conversations. So much time had been spent talking. They had talked about the sword, but now that was no help even with Riordan's records. David looked at the paper in Riordan's hand.

Wait. There's more.

David knew what would help. It was their last hope.

"Wait," David said. "Give us one more chance to prove my parents' true identity."

"And how will you accomplish this, David?" Morgana asked.

"The shield," he answered. Out of the corner of his eye, David saw his father, Mr. Linden, and Sir Garrett all perk up at this new suggestion. "The Shield of Faraman has been lost, correct?"

"No one has seen it in centuries," Garrett spoke up.

"I had it with me when we left," George added. "I think I can remember where we left it. Don't you, Tom?"

"It's worth a shot," Mr. Linden agreed.

"The only ones who would know where the Shield of Faraman might be and the only ones who would be able to bring it back would be the missing heirs, right?" David asked.

"Makes sense to me," Morgana answered before Lord Valstayne could object. "If you are able to return with the shield to match these records, I will have no choice but to step aside for the rightful heirs to this throne."

"Then we should go," Mr. Linden suggested.

"I'm coming with you," Sir Garrett offered.

"Since you seem so eager," Lord Valstayne observed, "to help these people whom you brought to take over the throne, I see it fitting that you join them. I had my suspicions you might be working with the rebels. Go then! However, Hannah will stay with us until your return."

David was not happy about this, but he did not see much of a choice.

"And," Valstayne added, "I believe we will hold Gretchen as well."

Guards grabbed Gretchen from her spot in line and moved her toward Hannah. "As collateral until all is decided." Garrett objected loudly, but there was nothing he could do. Not yet.

"David," Hannah spoke up, "think of what you are doing. I didn't last time you were here and look what's happened in Ethelrod. You can't just jump into things like before. Think things through, think of the consequences. Are you sure you want to go through with this? Forget about what happens to me, this might be too risky." Hannah really had grown in these past six months. The one who always dove in headfirst was now telling David to pause and reflect.

"I have been thinking about this," David answered. "I'm going to make whatever choices I can and face what consequences there are as long as I can get this country back on track and take you home safely." He glanced at Lord Valstayne and added, "No matter what obstacles are put in our way."

"By taking the girls, I'm just ensuring that you are doing what you say," Valstayne assured. He turned to Garrett. "All will be well if you stick to the plan and come back as quickly as possible. I am giving you three days to prove what these visitors say is true. I should hate to think what might happen should you be delayed or deviate from your current mission toward any other suspicious actions, Sir Garrett." Lord Valstayne made a gesture to the guards. "Take the girls away."

"Wait," Morgana interrupted. "You will see that these girls are kept comfortable." She turned to David. "I have faith you will succeed, and when you come back you will find them waiting for you. And until then, Elizabeth—"

"Yes?" she replied.

"I'll keep this seat warm for you."

"I appreciate it, Your Majesty."

It was decided that David, his parents, Mr. Linden, and Sir Garrett would all stay for the night and leave in the morning. They were given a lavish feast, new clothes, and comfortable quarters for a good night's rest before their journey.

David's room was right across the hall from his parents' room. While he was sure they were asleep, he was having trouble getting any rest. It had been quite an emotional day. A lot had happened. The future of the country was resting on this mission. Lying in bed thinking about the pressure was not helping him fall asleep any faster.

It also wasn't the quietest castle he had ever slept in. It was the only castle he had ever slept in, but still. The wind howled outside his window. He could hear the noises of men outside. His door creaked. David's ears focused on the sound. His door creaked when he opened it. Was someone opening his door? He turned in bed and watched as the latch moved, and the door slowly opened inward. Who would come to him in the middle of the night?

Is this another assassination attempt by Lord Valstayne?

David jumped out of bed, grabbed his sword, and braced it above his head ready to swing it down. He held his breath. A hooded figure entered the room. Just as David was about to swing, a pale hand reached out to stop him. David put down the sword and exhaled in relief. He threw the sword on his bed.

"Morgana, what are you doing here?"

"How did you know it was me?" she asked.

"Don't you have a habit of sneaking into my room wearing cloaks at night?" he joked.

"I guess I do." Morgana took off her cloak.

David saw a woman he had not seen in what felt like years to him and what were actually years to her. This Morgana was not the same. Her hair was behaving, and she looked cleaner and well-kept. This was the old version of her returned. Something must have happened to her deep inside during today's events to make this visible change.

"It was almost eleven years ago when I came to you in your room to ask you for a favor that would change my life. And here I am to do it again."

"What's wrong?" he asked.

"David, I need your story to be true."

"It is true, Morgana."

"Then, I need you to be able to prove it! Before, I asked you to help me gain some control in my life through that contest. Now, I am asking you to help me gain control of my whole life."

"What do you mean?"

"I am tired of this life I never chose for myself. I see that now. Of course, I have an obligation to my people to keep things in order while it is in my power and I will do so for as long as it takes. But if your family truly is the rightful heir to the throne, I want you to take it and quickly so I can start living my life for real. I know I am asking a lot."

"It's what we came here to do, to set things right. Knowing that you are rooting for us is encouraging."

"But it may be too dangerous. And it seems impossible that you will be able to find this needle in a haystack in just three days."

"Well, remember what you told me last time? 'Just because something is tough or difficult, it doesn't mean that it isn't possible.'"

Morgana smiled. "We are all rooting for you, David, even Lord Valstayne."

David was surprised. "Really?"

"Oh, yes. He is eager for you to begin your journey tomorrow."

"I bet he is. I just hope we can find what we are looking for and return safely."

"As do I," Morgana agreed. "I will do my best while you are gone, but I believe there are those better than I who can rule over Ethelrod. I would like to give your parents that chance to bring peace back to our kingdom and stop these wars."

"Thank you, Morgana."

"Good luck, David."

Chapter Twenty-five

David, his parents, Mr. Linden, and Garrett all met at the stables early the next morning. The stable boy brought Garrett his horse and four new ones were presented for the rest. They were eager to get a quick start. Sir Garrett looked stately as he got up on his horse. It was a simple search expedition, but he still wore his lighter set of armor as a leading member of the Guard. Mr. Linden and George also looked presentable in fine tunics, capes, riding pants, and boots that were similar to the ones David wore. His mother, however, looked odd for some reason.

"You're wearing that?" David asked.

Elizabeth was wearing a fine blouse with a cape to keep her warm, but she was also wearing riding pants and boots like the men. David didn't think he had ever seen a woman in Ethelrod wearing pants before, except when his friends and relatives showed up looking out of place.

Did any women wear pants in Ethelrod?

"The ladies who tried to dress me this morning almost wouldn't let me leave," she said. "But I told them that I was going to ride a horse, and I was going to do it with one leg on each side of the saddle. I also told them that if I am going to scour the countryside, then there was no way I was going to do so in a dress. They had a fit, but as you can see, I won."

"Bravo, Elizabeth," Mr. Linden said, laughing.

"Shall we?" Garrett asked, motioning toward the street that would circle the castle wall to the front gate and lead them to the town square.

"Let's go," said George, as he gave his horse a soft kick and moved forward.

"Where are we going anyway?" David asked. "Are you sure you know where to look after all this time?"

"We are going to the Northern Mountains."

"What? The mountain range you said only yesterday was too dangerous for any man and might even have dragons. That's where we're going?"

"It's where we were when Mr. Linden closed the book and we left Ethelrod," Elizabeth answered. "That's where the sword and the shield were left behind. It's our best chance of finding the shield."

"Besides, David," Garrett explained, "treasure-seekers are only a myth. They don't exist."

"Oh, yes they do," Mr. Linden contradicted. Garrett looked stunned. "My boys, why do you think we left Ethelrod all the way in the Northern Mountains? It's because I lost the book and had to get it back. I'll give you one guess if you can figure out who took it."

"A treasure-seeker?" David answered.

"Impossible!" Garrett protested.

"Quite possible," Mr. Linden replied. "My only hope is that the shield is still in the clearing where we left it, covered and hidden by centuries of forest growth. That would be much better than if it has gotten into the hands of a treasure-seeker who has sniffed it out and claimed it as his own."

"Then we better get a move on," George announced.

The gate opened, letting them out into the town square of the High Kingdom. They double-checked that they had all of their supplies and were ready to go before racing off toward the north. Three days did not seem like that much time, but they had to do what they could. Hannah's and Gretchen's safety were on the line.

The traveling pack moved at a quick pace but still left time to rest the horses, take water from the stream, and do what they needed. In the group, David was the least comfortable on a horse, but he hid it well. His legs and backside ached, but there were more important things to think about. And besides, if Garrett could do this inside a tin can, then he could do it in pants without complaining.

"I still can't get over the fact that treasure-seekers are real," Garrett continued. "I mean, everyone has heard about them, but only from old tales. We figured they were fake or had all died out years ago."

"Well, you can tell that to a treasure-seeker when you see one and see what he says," Mr. Linden responded.

"Talk to it? They speak the same language as us?" Garrett looked stunned.

"They could talk for hours if they had a mind to," Mr. Linden answered.

"That's just it," George added. "They have to be in the mood to talk. You don't want to catch them when they're, well—"

"What?" Garrett asked.

David could figure it out. "Hungry."

George nodded.

"Now, now," Mr. Linden started. "You just need to know how a treasure-seeker thinks, figure out what he wants, and how to approach the creature."

"You speak as if you are an expert," Elizabeth said.

"Yeah, so?"

"You've only ever met one!" Elizabeth called him out.

"Well, it worked then and it can work now if we must come to it."

"Tom, you don't even know if the shield has been taken by a treasure-seeker yet. And besides, the one nice treasure-seeker you interacted with to get your book back may not even be alive anymore. It was ages ago."

"Treasure-seekers only want one thing," Mr. Linden replied. "Booty, and as much as they can find."

George interrupted. "All this treasure-seeker talk. Let's wait to cross that bridge until we have to."

"You're kind of like a treasure-seeker yourself, Tom," Elizabeth joked.

"How's that?"

"You also seek treasure and try to get as much as you can."

"I may be richer than some back home, have a nice house and whatnot, but that in no way makes me a treasure-seeker. Most of that is just family money."

"I'm not talking about family money. I'm talking about that book of yours."

"Don't be ridiculous."

"You treat that book as if it were a treasure. It's a precious object to be sure, but you use it to collect more treasure." David could see Mr. Linden wanted to interrupt, but his mother continued. "You use it to collect experiences. You travel and explore and have to keep going until you've collected all there is to see, hear, and touch."

"I guess, but a treasure-seeker, really?"

"Since you've been back, you haven't been able to travel. Weren't you a little bit jealous when you found out the book worked for David and not you? Don't you want to fix this situation so the book will work as it used to?" Elizabeth asked.

"You're upset that I want to explore new worlds? Experiencing life is a bad thing?"

"It is when collecting experiences is more important than your personal responsibilities."

"I do not shirk responsibilities."

"Would the daughter who ran away from home have the same

answer to that question?" Elizabeth might have gone too far. What started out as a simple joke unleashed some underlying tension between the two.

"Responsibility! Funny, coming from the woman who ran away from the country she was supposed to rule," Mr. Linden jabbed.

"And look who's back trying to save it!"

"Enough!" George yelled. "This argument has gone on long enough. We all made mistakes in the past, but the future is what we need to be focusing on now. We need to—"

George didn't finish because a black arrow landed in his left shoulder and knocked him off his horse to the ground.

Chapter Twenty-six

"George!"

Elizabeth quickly got off her horse, ran to him, and knelt by his side. Mr. Linden, Garrett, and David jumped off their horses and hid behind trees to shield themselves from the wave of arrows shooting in their direction. Garrett tried to advance forward but was unable. David tried, but an arrow whizzed by his face, and he took cover again.

As quickly as it started, it stopped.

"They must be out of arrows," Garrett supposed. They all listened closely. Three sets of feet were heard getting off their horses. They were walking closer. Without talking, Garrett, David, and Mr. Linden all followed the same plan. Garrett was the first to take out his sword. Then David. Then Mr. Linden. David noticed his sword looked a bit different. Mr. Linden cursed.

"What's wrong? What is that?" David whispered.

"Wood," Mr. Linden answered. "It's a dummy. Must have been given to me by one of Valstayne's men."

Elizabeth took out George's sword and it was the same. Two swords against three men. Garrett moved forward and hid behind the next tree.

"David," Mr. Linden called quietly, "give me your sword."

"Sorry, no." And before Mr. Linden or his mother could object, David advanced like Garrett to the next tree.

The two of them moved forward and out silently as the three attackers worked toward them, making plenty of noise. Garrett was now farther away but still in line with David. David backed up to the last tree and waited. The footsteps were almost upon them now. A snapping branch signaled that one was right on the other side of the tree trunk. He looked to Garrett for guidance, but Garrett was gone.

David knelt in a crouched position and held up his sword. Soft rustling drew closer. He felt a soft pain in his chest and then remembered to breathe. David just needed a little glimpse.

Does the opponent know I'm behind this tree waiting for him?

Is the opponent waiting for me?

The rustling moved a few inches closer.

Come on, come on, David thought. *Get this over with.*

A few more inches closer.

Then it happened. David could see the front half of his opponent's foot as it came around the tree. With all his might, David thrust his sword down into the attacker's foot and well into the ground. The man's scream filled the forest. David then heard the clashing of metal that meant Garrett was now in combat as well.

The armored man swung his sword in David's direction, but David had already rolled to the side and out of his reach. He would have taken his sword with him, but it was in there pretty deep. The man locked eyes with David through his face mask and reached down to the hilt of David's sword. Slowly, he pulled it out of the ground and out of his foot. David could see blood on the blade. The man threw the weapon to the side and limped toward David. This man must have been in peak physical condition because even with an injured foot, he was limping pretty quickly.

David turned and tripped over a large root, falling to the ground. The attacker came toward him, raising his sword for a deadly blow. David tried to scramble backward, but the leafy ground slowed him down. The opponent was upon him, took aim, and started to swing his blade.

David shut his eyes and waited for pain, but it never came. Instead he heard a large splitting noise, and David opened his eyes. Mr. Linden blocked the blow with his wooden sword, but the force of the blow shattered it so that only a sharp stump remained. This surprise defense stunned the attacker, but Mr. Linden was not taken aback.

Swiftly, he used the sharp broken edge of his now-useful weapon and stuck it into the stranger's throat, right between where the face mask met the breastplate. Blood trickled out onto the clean silver armor and gurgling noises could be heard as the man crumpled to the ground at David's feet. David wanted to throw up, but there was no time.

"David!" Mr. Linden shouted. "Get a move on!"

David ran to where he thought his sword was thrown and searched through the plant growth. Garrett was fighting his opponent in the distance. His six months in the Castle Guard starting up a rebellion had served him well. David could see why he was now a captain; Garrett was skilled. David continued to search for the sword, thrashing through the ferns.

"Look out!" Mr. Linden called.

The third and final attacker came toward him.

"Where is my sword?" David said.

The new opponent ran forward and whipped out his weapon to run David through. Just in time, David's hand felt the hard, cold metal of his sword. He sliced his sword through the air and parried the attacker's blow as he ran past. The opponent turned around and David stood up tall to face him. The attacker came closer and dealt three quick movements, all of which David deflected with ease.

Back at Mr. Linden's house, David would try to practice with this same sword, but it was always forced and clumsy. Here, it was easy and graceful. Either David's practice was now paying off with thanks to his adrenaline from the moment, or there was something about him being in Ethelrod that brought out his best abilities not seen back home.

"Is that all you got?" David taunted.

Two more defensive moves and the attacker was now behind him. David started some offensive maneuvers and drew the attacker back away from Mr. Linden and his parents. David slashed horizontally, but the opponent jumped backward. In David's follow-through, the opponent made to strike vertically, attempting to bring his sword down on David's skull. David used the momentum on his last move to keep spinning and the blow missed him. He then moved his sword up, but it was knocked back down. David's next blow went off his opponent's armor.

"David! Protect yourself!" Mr. Linden advised.

He took a few steps back and went on the defensive again. David's horizontal slash missed again, and again the opponent made for the vertical blow. This time, David used his momentum to turn and instead of rolling away, he thrust his sword behind him for a backward blow that landed in the soft spot exposed on the opponent's left side. The attacker groaned in pain and dropped the sword from his hands raised above his head. David turned around to see the man fall onto his back and hold his side tight.

Garrett came over to check out the situation.

"All good here?" Garrett asked.

"Yes, but my dad!"

George was breathing heavily in pain, but he said he was fine. Mr. Linden was preparing to take the arrow out of his shoulder. David could hear Garrett take the helmet off of the injured man and his troubled breathing and coughing became louder.

"Oh, my God," Garrett said.

David recognized the face of one of the attackers. It was Andrew, the member of the Castle Guard who opened the gates the previous day when Garrett brought David and the others to see the queen.

"What the heck are you doing, Andrew?" Garrett asked.

Andrew struggled to respond. David had injured him pretty badly. David looked at the familiar arrow in his dad's shoulder and called to his friend. "Garrett, look at this arrow."

"A red boar?"

Elizabeth looked up questioningly.

"Valstayne," David answered.

Andrew tried to explain. "He said he would harm our families if we refused. We had no choice."

"I understand," Garrett comforted. The man was dying. "Andrew, I promise I will do my best to protect them." He nodded in appreciation. "Andrew, stay with me! You are going to be fine. We are going to get you on your horse, and you are going to ride straight to the Western Shore. Do you understand me?" Andrew was groggy, so it was unclear how much he comprehended. "You are going to ride for the Western Shore and look for my father. He will keep you safe until this is all over."

Garrett struggled but got Andrew slumped back onto his horse. Garrett hit the horse hard and it sped off west.

"Do you think he'll make it?"

"We can only hope," Garrett replied.

David got up and walked toward Garrett. "I'm so sorry."

Garrett waved it off. "It was Valstayne. He's responsible for my friends, for all of this."

George screamed as Mr. Linden pulled out the arrow. Elizabeth efficiently packed the wound with supplies she'd brought with them. George sat up as Elizabeth put his arm into a makeshift sling.

"Why would Lord Valstayne do this?" George asked.

"He'd do anything to keep Morgana in power. That's where he gets his control," David answered. "This isn't the first time he tried to have me killed."

"But he gave us three days," Elizabeth said.

"I should have known," David said. "Morgana mentioned Valstayne was eager for us to begin our journey. This must have been why—so he could plan his attack away from the castle."

"And if the attack had been successful," Garrett finished, "then it would just look like we went missing on a dangerous mission and no one would think anything else."

"But when we didn't return," Mr. Linden started. "The girls—"

"He would have had them killed," David replied.

"This man is the devil," George concluded.

"We have to go back and stop him," Elizabeth suggested.

"The only way to do that is to find the shield and get back as quickly as possible," George replied.

"Then we need to get going," Mr. Linden said. "Now, even."

"We're camping here for the night," Garrett said firmly. There were plenty of objections to this. "George needs to get his strength back. We have two more days to do what we need to do, and it won't help if we are all tired. Take the night and reenergize, get supplies, make camp. For me, I'm going to bury my friends."

Mr. Linden started setting up sleeping arrangements. George used his good arm and unpacked some food they had brought along. Elizabeth went in search of wood to start a fire.

As Garrett walked away, David called, "Wait! I'll help you."

David and Garrett buried the two fallen men of the Castle Guard.

Chapter Twenty-seven

The next morning, they all rose early. Lying on the stiff ground didn't offer much possibility for sleeping comfortably anyway. They packed up camp silently and continued north. They left the outer rim of the woods and were making their climb up into the Northern Mountains. David was unsure if Mr. Linden or his parents knew exactly where they were going until they reached a wide and rocky dry riverbed.

"This is good," George said. "We just need to follow this river north and we should be fine."

"What river?" David asked.

"It fills up in the spring when the mountain snow melts," Elizabeth explained. "It's the river we followed to find the book last time."

"When you were tracking the treasure-seeker," Garrett added.

"Well, yes."

Garrett's sword remained in its sheath, but he grasped the hilt firmly at his waist.

They continued until the uninhabited woods got so dense that they had to dismount their horses and walk on foot. Elizabeth suggested that David and Garrett try below in the rocky, uneven riverbed while the three remaining fought through the vegetation. David and Garrett didn't mind.

After a while, David could hear his parents talking with Mr. Linden. Soon their voices were raised as if they were fighting with each other again. He couldn't quite make out what they said. David tried to focus on the words, but navigating the riverbed and trying to lead his horse along required too much of his attention.

Above the riverbed, the adults were in a heated discussion.

"Yes, I would like to be king again," George admitted, "but I also think it is our duty to fix what we left."

"Our duty?" Elizabeth questioned.

"Because we left, this has all been allowed to happen. Who knows where Ethelrod could be by now if we had stayed? It is our responsibility to stay this time and do what we were born to do."

"Born to do? What about our son? What was he born to do? Give up his life to follow the footsteps of his parents? Give up his personal dreams for our own desires? That is the reason we left in the first place, George!"

"Elizabeth," Tom interrupted, "think of the progress you could bring to Ethelrod. This land has remained unchanged in your absence. Yet now, here you are with a world of knowledge to bring back and use to help move this world forward."

"Again, what about David?" she asked. "He was not born here. It isn't his responsibility to stay when he could have a better life elsewhere."

"Maybe you're right," George said. "Maybe this is not David's world. David is growing up. Maybe his path is in a world separate from his parents, so that he can grow to his full potential without us."

"What are you saying? I can't talk about this. I don't think I could do that, especially not when our only option is him." She motioned to Tom. "'Uncle Tom' is the reason we are here now. We sent David away to avoid all this and here we are."

Elizabeth stormed ahead of them.

"She's right, Tom," George added. "It's no use if we can't trust you to take some responsibility, too. You have to be responsible for Hannah, more so than before she ran away. I need to know you won't get obsessed in your book and get lost again, forgetting about everybody else. Can you do that, Tom? Be the man we need you to be?"

Before Tom could respond, Elizabeth called out from ahead. "Hey! You have to see this! I think this is it!"

They quickly joined her in a small clearing where a twisted black tree was visible. George felt the charred edges where the tree had been struck by lightning and split in two. Elizabeth was right. This was it. She hoped the shield was near.

The next thing David could make out was his father's voice calling to them. "David! Garrett! Over here!"

Eventually, David and Garrett managed to find their way out of the deep riverbed and regroup with the others. They found them in a clearing, searching.

"Are we here? Is this it?" Garrett asked.

"We're here," Mr. Linden answered. "Look around. And look hard, it could be anywhere after all these years, even partially or fully buried."

"How do you know this is the spot?" David wondered.

"See that tree?" Elizabeth pointed out a large, mangled tree. "It's been split in two by lightning. This is the spot where we left Ethelrod with Mr. Linden. We're sure of it."

They searched for hours, but it was no use. They tried fanning out in a larger radius. They even tried digging in several places, but the shield could not be found. Everyone was getting tired and frustrated.

"You know what we have to do," Mr. Linden finally said.

"I hoped we wouldn't have to," George replied.

"It's our only option left."

"What?" David asked. "What are we going to do?"

"We need to find Azreal," Mr. Linden answered.

"Who's Azreal?" Garrett asked.

"A treasure-seeker."

Chapter Twenty-eight

David was surprised at how much his parents and Mr. Linden remembered about the area. Thanks to the lightning tree, they were able to get their bearings and knew exactly where to go to find Azreal. At a certain point, they tied off their horses and went forward without them. They climbed higher into the Northern Mountains and crossed dangerously high paths that David wished had railings or at least a caution sign. More than once, David imagined himself accidentally tripping and falling into the abyss below. It was better to keep his mind off it and constantly double-and triple-check his next step.

They made their way down a mountain and into a grassy valley, also heavily wooded like the forest on the other side. It was like a little section of the forest had been taken out and placed in the middle of a room that had mountains as walls. Mr. Linden and David's parents started circling the large rock-walled perimeter of the woods searching for something particular. Garrett and David followed.

Eventually, the group found their way to a large cave entrance. To the untrained eye, it might've appeared as if a random rockslide had placed these stones here with a large hole in the middle, but the boulders fit too nicely together to be there by accident.

"This is it," Mr. Linden announced. "This is the entrance to Azreal's hoard."

They took off their packs and George made torches out of some sticks, fabric, and a liquid from their supplies. "It's going to be dark in there," George said. "And we don't want any surprises."

"What if Azreal doesn't live here anymore?" David questioned. "Or what if he's not the dragon you knew him to be so long ago?"

"Azreal's hoard is one of the largest collections of treasure of any treasure-seeker. I doubt he would risk moving it," Elizabeth said. "As for that second question, we'll just have to go and find out."

George passed out the torches. They all made their way through the large, shadowy entrance and down the path that led into the base of the mountain to Azreal.

Here and there, David would find a few gold coins or a golden goblet with precious gems lying on the path as if forgotten. "Azreal's treasure must be incredible for him to leave these behind," David guessed.

"You have no idea," said Mr. Linden.

They kept walking down the winding path that became darker and darker the deeper they went into the earth. They went on and on until suddenly they came to a dead end in a small cave. They felt around with their hands and searched with their torches, but it truly was closed off.

"This can't be," Mr. Linden said.

"There has to be a way through," George replied.

"Maybe it caved in," Garrett suggested.

They continued to search the cave. David knocked on the hard, cold stone, hoping to find some kind of secret passage that would let them continue forward. All of the places he knocked were solid. However, his last knock offered back a different type of sound, not exactly hollow but not as solid as the stone before. He knocked again, harder. The same sound returned. "I think I've found something."

But when David turned back to the wall, he was no longer looking at stone but at a huge yellow eyeball almost the size of his body. The eye searched back and forth until it focused on David and his torch, and the eye's pupil contracted.

"David, get back!" his dad yelled.

The entire wall of rock in front of David seemed to shake and move. The eye rose up along the wall. More rocks shifted and then there were two eyes staring down at David as he backed away quickly. Were David's own eyes playing tricks on him, or did the moving rocks seem to form an outline? He could barely make it out, but he kept coming to the same conclusion. Was Azreal the treasure-seeker made out of rock?

"Is that him?" he asked.

The rock wall stepped toward them.

"Azreal?" Mr. Linden called.

The wall stopped.

From an open space that somewhat resembled a mouth, a low voice came, "How do you know that name?"

"We have been here before, spoken with you, traded with you. You may not remember us; it was centuries ago," Mr. Linden explained.

"Are you not human?" the creature asked.

"We are," George answered.

"Then it is impossible that we met centuries before. Humans do not live as long as us treasure-seekers."

Elizabeth took her turn. "Azreal, the last time we were here, I traded my mother's necklace for a red book with golden pages. It was that book that transported us to a world where time moves slower than it does here. So you see, it is really us."

"This necklace," Azreal started, "what did it look like?"

"An elaborate fish, the symbol of my mother's house, with pearl scales and sapphire eyes."

"I remember it well," Azreal recollected. "It was an easy trade for something as simple and as plain as a book."

"Books can be treasure, too," David said before he realized what he was doing.

"But they have no value."

"They can improve your mind, help you grow as an individual. Books can be used to share ideas and experiences with as many people as possible. As a reader, you have a chance to go on adventures you never might have even imagined before. Books hold connections between us all. It's a great treasure to read something that you thought was a feeling only you had but can find it there written on a page by someone else. Haven't you ever felt that when you read?"

"Treasure-seekers don't read," Azreal responded shortly. "However, I might be able to see your point, even though I don't agree with something so strictly human."

"Azreal," Mr. Linden said. "We have come for some help. We are looking for something and were hoping to see if you had it with you. If you do, we would like to talk."

"This interests me," Azreal said, delightedly. He rapidly shook his body and the stones fell away. The edges of Azreal's body seemed blurry and for a moment he seemed to transition into something else.

"What the—" Garrett started, but George cut him off.

"Treasure-seekers are masters of disguise. It's how they've been able to remain a myth for so long."

As Azreal shifted appearances, David was reminded of the brief moment of static one sees when moving between television channels. Azreal stopped moving and there he stood in what David figured to be his true, bright, colorful self.

Azreal was not the horned, winged dragon with flaming nostrils that David had grown up hearing about in his storybooks. Instead, Azreal resembled the types of dragons David saw on menus and placemats at Chinese restaurants. His head was large, with gold pointy ears on either side of his face. The whiskers from his snout were also golden, almost matching his yellow eyes. His body was long and scaly, with four legs that ended in sharp silver claws. David noticed that Azreal's feet never really touched the ground; he just hovered in the air as his body slithered back and forth, up and down.

He had gold-detailed extensions around his knees and elbows or whatever you called them in dragon anatomy. Azreal was covered in brilliant scales that glowed in the presence of their torches below. The scales were a combination of ruby red and emerald green and shifted depending on the angle of the scale as the creature was moving. Azreal was a shimmering treasure himself. David stood in awe.

"What is it you seek?" Azreal asked.

"We would like to take a look at your hoard to see if a bit of treasure called the Shield of Faraman has made its way to your collection," Mr. Linden explained.

"No," came the quick answer. "Why do you think I am hiding here, guarding my treasure instead of taking pleasure in it?" The group remained silent. "Only a few years ago, very recent for treasure-seekers, a human came into my hoard and took something that belonged to me." Garrett shifted uncomfortably in his spot and took a quick sidestep closer to David. "Since then, I have been standing guard for thieves, so no, you do not get to walk into my hoard at your pleasure."

"This is understandable," Mr. Linden agreed. "And we would never wish to leave with something without your consent. Therefore, we humbly ask to be allowed to leave with the Shield of Faraman should you have it in your possession."

"And what would I get in return?" Azreal asked.

"I'm afraid," George said, "that this time we do not have anything of value to trade. That shield was a family heirloom that was passed down to me. Right now, it is the only thing that can prove my lineage in order to take back Ethelrod with my wife and attempt to lead it into a time of peace."

"And you think you could be capable of such an accomplishment?"

George looked at Elizabeth and was quiet for a moment. "I am not sure, but it is my responsibility to try."

"A solid answer, but that situation has little to do with me. I have seen multiple times of war and peace changing like the tides. I hold little faith in the responsibilities of man."

"I cannot speak for others who may come after me, but I can assure you that as long as I live and remain in control, I will do whatever is necessary to see that Ethelrod continues to progress and flourish."

"And a simple shield can start this course?" Azreal doubted.

"Yes, exactly," George answered.

Azreal considered this. "I will see if I have it in my hoard, but it does not change the fact that you have nothing of value to trade for it."

"We will talk about that while you look," Mr. Linden suggested.

Seemingly content with this option, Azreal turned in the spot where he hovered above the ground and made to move deeper into the cave.

Elizabeth spoke up. "Excuse me." Azreal faced her. "I was wondering if I might be able to just see my mother's necklace. The fish one? If it wouldn't be too much trouble."

"I do not have that anymore," he said. "I traded it for—" Azreal stopped for a moment. "For something that you might be able to help me with in exchange for the shield."

"If you have it," Garrett added.

"Of course I have it," Azreal replied. "A treasure-seeker always knows every single piece of treasure inside his collection."

Azreal left and returned shortly after, slithering through the air. Before them, he placed a bright silver shield emblazoned with a crimson stag standing upright, presenting its forward hooves and antlers as ready for battle.

"That's it!" David said, as he went forward to claim it.

A bright set of claws stopped him where he was. "Not so fast," Azreal said. "The shield is yours only if you can help me out."

"How do we do that?" David asked.

Azreal pushed forward a silver cube and said to Elizabeth, "I traded your mother's necklace with a man who said that this box, of his own design, held the greatest treasure anyone could ever hope to possess. However, the box is locked, and I cannot open it. I believe it is a puzzle, but cannot figure it out or maneuver the box with my claws." He flashed his silver talons at them. "If you can open this box and reveal the treasure inside, then the shield is yours."

Everyone got closer and circled the box. All six silver sides were the same shape. There was a top that seemed to be clasped shut. The clasp looked like a male human face, and it seemed that the box would open where the mouth was. Garrett pulled at this spot, but the bottom and the top would not separate. On two opposite sides, next to the face, there were circles with animals engraved inside them.

"This one is cute," Elizabeth said, pointing at the bear. As she touched the circle, it popped out and lay on the ground. "Oh!"

"It's okay," George said. "It looks as if these are supposed to come out."

Elizabeth picked up the one she knocked out. "Look. It's engraved and flat on one side, but the other has this weird carving on the back."

"Almost like it fits into something," David added. "Look at the top here." David pointed to four circular indentations at the four corners of the top surrounding both a sun and a moon. "It looks like they are supposed to fit in here."

"Very good, David," said his father, impressed.

"But which four," Elizabeth wondered, as she counted the circles of animals. There were five circles on each of the two sides, ten total.

"This might help," Mr. Linden said. "Here on the back is an inscription." He read it out loud:

"In this box, there is a treasure inside;
one so precious it is a crime to hide.
No strong force shall open it;
use your mind to interpret it.
The directions are in these words:
group the animals into herds.
Four keys in the wilderness lie,
each must go to its spot, no retry.
The spinning orb will open doors,
and the treasure at last shall be yours."

"It is a puzzle!" Azreal seemed satisfied with himself for knowing it all along.

"And the poem here tells us how to get into the box," David continued. He turned to Azreal, "See, it is useful to know how to read."

Azreal snorted at him.

"Okay," George reasoned, "it seems like we get only one shot at this. 'No retry.' Elizabeth! Good thing we have you; you love puzzles!"

Everyone stared at Elizabeth. David knew this fact to be true. His mother loved pouring out the contents of a puzzle and running her fingers along the cardboard shapes. She had done so many; they were like child's play to her, no matter how many pieces the picture was divided into, no matter how intricately cut the shapes of the puzzle happened to be. Elizabeth always made David work with her on puzzles whether he wanted to or not, always reminding him to look at the details while not forgetting the big picture.

"This isn't a normal jigsaw puzzle, George. I don't know if I can do this. And we get only one shot." She backed away from the box.

"Elizabeth, take a breath." He rubbed her arms to calm her down. "I know you can do this. We all do."

"You got this, Mom," David reassured her.

Elizabeth stepped up to the box and knelt down beside it. David and George joined her, while Mr. Linden and Garrett paced around them. Elizabeth took out the remaining animals and examined them. "A bear. A snake. A lion. A wolf. A fish. A bird. A squirrel. This one is either a turtle or a tortoise; I hope it doesn't matter. A whale it looks like and an insect, probably a fly."

"What a random collection," David commented.

"It looks like we have to group them together into some type of herd. What do they all have in common?" George asked.

"These animals couldn't be any more different from each other, Dad."

"Then how are we going to do this?"

Elizabeth was thinking silently and went to reread the poem

again. "'Four keys in the wilderness lie,' which means that these wild animals are the keys, but we need to find out which four." She kept reading and rereading. She whispered to herself, "I don't want to get this wrong."

She looked again at the animals. "What if we don't have to group them into one common family?" she suggested.

"But it says we must put them into a herd," George stated.

"No," Elizabeth corrected. "It says we must divide them into herds. Plural. What if we just look for the animals that travel in packs?"

"Well, that would give us the wolf," David answered. "A group of wolves is called a pack."

"What else can we find?" George asked.

"Look for your collective nouns," she said. "David's right; we want the wolf because wolves travel in packs. We can use the lion, a pride, the fish, which travel in a school, and the bird, a flock."

"Sounds good to me," George said. "Throw them in there."

"But into which spots?" Elizabeth was still thinking.

David held the wolf in his hand. He felt the grooves on the back that looked like they fit like gears into their places at the top of the box. All of the gears were exactly the same, so any could go into the spots. Maybe the clue was with the picture itself. The wolf on the metal coin looked simple enough. He ran his finger over the raised image of the animal. His finger also felt something else. Behind the wolf was an intricate web of lines and loops. He looked at the top of the box, which had a similar pattern. David held up the wolf next to the top left empty place. The lines matched.

"Look at this, Mom! The design in the background matches the coin. We just have to match up the backgrounds!"

Elizabeth studied the background of the wolf and agreed energetically that it could fit in that spot. She also held up the lion next to the same place and became more sober. "This one would fit, too," she said regretfully. "It was a good idea, David."

David had thought he was so close to figuring out the puzzle and saving the day. Close? If his mother hadn't been here, he never would have even gotten past the poem. She was the puzzle person in the family. Again, David remembered her constantly telling him to look at the details and not forget the whole picture. The whole picture! David looked again at the animal medallions and the top of the box. It was true all the lines and loops were the same, but not quite. You had to look at the whole picture.

"Here we go, Mom," David said. "We know we have to match the background design to the design on the box. It's very detailed, but take a step back and look at the top of the box as a whole. What do you see?"

Elizabeth stared hard at the box. She looked at the coins and then back at the box again. "David, that's it!"

"What's it?" George asked.

Elizabeth explained. "There is one spinning line, see it here?" Elizabeth traced its path around the box.

"What about it?"

"It's darker and deeper than the rest. Not by much, but still, the difference is there and just enough to help us place the animals in their proper places."

David fit the wolf into the lower right circle and the different lines matched up perfectly. Elizabeth put the lion in the top right and the fish into the bottom left, while George placed the last key into the top left place. All of the pieces matched perfectly. George smiled and softly ran his hand over the top of the box.

"Will it open now?" asked Garrett, who had been watching patiently.

"Not just yet," Elizabeth said. "We need the spinning orb."

George tapped the sun. "This looks like a moving piece here. Let's give it a crank, open it on up, and get on out of here."

George reached for the sun, but David grabbed his wrist to stop him. "No." David looked at his mom and Elizabeth nodded to him. "The sun and moon both move, but we want the spinning orb. The

planets move around the sun, but the moon is the one that spins."
Who knew that chapter in science class would end up being useful?

"It's true even in Ethelrod," Elizabeth said.

David placed his fingers on the moon and slowly turned it clock-wise. Tiny clinking gears moved as the four animals also spun in their place. David had almost spun the moon halfway when a final click caused the chin to drop on the clasp that was a man's face. They had unlocked the box.

Elizabeth turned the box toward Azreal, and he hovered closer to look. Elizabeth lifted off the top of the box, and it split the clasp as if the man were yawning. Or singing. As the box was fully open, a repetition of tinkles and twinkles began to play a soft lullaby.

"It's a music box," realized Mr. Linden.

"The treasure is music?" Garrett questioned. "Doesn't seem worth it to me."

David watched Azreal sway silently in time to the music. The treasure-seeker really enjoyed the music.

"Isn't it beautiful?"

Chapter Twenty-nine

David blinked and shielded his eyes from the bright sun as he exited the cave and stepped back into the forest in the valley ridge of the Northern Mountains. His eyes adjusted, and he lowered his hand to the leather strap across his chest that meant the impressive Shield of Faraman was still strapped to his back. The rest of the group came out of the cave after him.

"I can't believe the treasure was music," Garrett continued.

"Treasure can be different for different people," Elizabeth explained. "It could be music or gold."

"Or books," David added, looking back at Azreal.

As a body part of the treasure-seeker crossed the threshold of the cave, the shimmering ruby and emerald scales shone and then were replaced with the three-dimensional vertical brown and black stripes of the bark of the surrounding trees. He blended right in.

"Or experience," said Mr. Linden.

"Or family," added George. He pressed Elizabeth close to him.

"Or love," Garrett said.

"We need to get back to the High Kingdom to help Hannah and Gretchen," Mr. Linden announced.

"We have plenty of time," George said. "Look at the sun."

Elizabeth frantically searched the sky. "We entered the cave in the afternoon and the sun was to the left. It's now on the right! We were in the cave longer than we thought. It's not afternoon; it's morning! Of the third day!"

"We have to go now!" Garrett yelled. He raced back to the path that would lead to where they tied the horses.

"We'll never make it," Mr. Linden said worriedly. "We have a two-day journey to make!"

David turned to the treasure-seeker. "Azreal, you don't think you could—"

"I don't give rides," he interjected. "You'd better get going."

Azreal went back to the cave and his hoard.

David, his mother, and father turned and ran to catch up with Garrett and Mr. Linden, who had more to lose for their tardiness.

Can we make it back to the High Kingdom in time?

David knew they had to try.

They urged the horses beneath them to go as fast as they could. Trees whipped by them in a flash. The scenery sped by in pieces, as if on a projector set to fast forward. If David could feel his horse slowing down, he urged it on even more. David was the one with the shield on his back. He was the important one who had to make it.

The five travelers finally made it to the edge of the woods where they could see the High Kingdom in the distance. David enjoyed this familiar view, but they had no time to spare.

"We made it," George announced, as it was still light out.

"Not quite," Elizabeth corrected. She motioned with her head toward the direction of the sun, which had just touched the tip of a hill in the distance. Sunset was starting.

David kicked his horse and rode on as fast as possible.

"Where are they?" Gretchen whispered.

"They will be here soon," Hannah assured her.

I hope, Hannah thought.

Hannah and Gretchen knelt in the center of the Great Hall in front of the throne platform. They had been given fine new dresses to wear during their captivity, but it was of little concern to them as they stared out the stained glass windows and watched the sun start to sink below the horizon.

The courtiers surrounded them, but they did not get too close. No one stood up for the pair of young girls whose lives were apparently at stake. No one knew how to behave in such a situation. Morgana and Lord Valstayne were audibly fighting at the front of the hall.

"Three days was not enough time!" Morgana pleaded. "You must give an extension."

"They knew the arrangement," Lord Valstayne argued. "They should have turned back when they could if they knew what was good for our guests." He stared down at Hannah, and she looked at him right back into his gray eye that was the center of the pink scar that ran down the side of his face.

"I will not have them harmed," Morgana ordered.

"Your Majesty," Valstayne explained, "the suspicious Sir Garrett could be rallying up rebel troops to storm the castle as we speak. This will not stand and collateral damage will be dealt with so all of Ethelrod knows who they are dealing with."

"But Valstayne," Morgana tried again.

"No extensions will be given!"

A voice called from the back. "No extension will be necessary!"

Hannah smiled. *David!*

The crowd parted as David, Mr. Linden, Sir Garrett, George, and Elizabeth all walked toward the front of the Great Hall. Gretchen got up and ran into Garrett's arms and Hannah went to her father. David walked straight up to Morgana and Valstayne, took the shield off his back, and held it in the air.

"Here!"

"Look!" a female member of the court cried out. Everyone in the room followed her ringed finger and saw the sun sink below the horizon.

"Right on time," David said.

"Valstayne, in their absence, I have been working with Riordan, and I believe everything these people say to be true. If faith alone does not prove it, then this presentation of the shield does. David's parents are the rightful heirs to the throne, and I wish to step down," Morgana stated plainly.

"Who do you think you are?" Valstayne spat his words at her. "I raised you on this throne. You will do exactly what I say, and you are staying where you are. I kept you in power during this time of war."

"Even if it meant killing her fiancé and any other eligible suitor?" David accused.

Morgana looked shocked. "Is this true? You are the reason behind this madness?"

"I have done what needs to be done!" Valstayne yelled. "And I will not have you ruin this for us."

"The throne is not mine. I do not wish to fight to keep a life I no longer even want." Morgana tried to reason with him.

"Well, I want it! I have the real power, the armies, and the control. And I will not let you just give it away."

"Lord Valstayne," Morgana corrected, "I am the one with the power here. As long as I am the one on the throne, I have the control. You are dismissed of your position. I no longer require your services."

David no longer saw the crazed frantic queen from a few months ago. He saw the powerful woman he once knew coming back.

Valstayne laughed at her. "You think that sitting in a special chair gives you power? Ha! Real power belongs to the one who pays the armies and that would be me. Members of the Castle Guard," he called, "seize them!"

Guards drew their weapons and came to surround them. However, this was not something unexpected by the group. Mr. Linden, Sir Garrett, and George sheltered their female companions and rushed them out of the hall. David ran up to Morgana and grabbed her by the hand.

"Time to go," he ordered, as he pulled her away from Valstayne and out of the Great Hall with the others.

They made it out to the courtyard. "What is going on?" Morgana asked. "Where are we going?"

"We just have to make it back to the town square outside the gates," David said.

"We have a plan," Garrett assured.

"But it all relies on us making it out alive," George added.

More guards were exiting the castle. Word had spread to the others that they were wanted.

With no time to stop for the horses, they ran toward the winding path that followed the outer castle wall to the front gate. Guards ran after them on the tops of the walls. Some even started shooting arrows from the platforms above. No one stopped running. They were almost to the gate.

When they reached it, they hid from arrows under the arch as Garrett attempted to raise the portcullis. It wasn't happening as quickly as was necessary. David used the shield on his back to protect him as he went to help Garrett. He was glad he had the shield because he heard an arrow bounce off the metal. David and Garrett raised the portcullis just enough to usher everyone out to the safety that lay on the other side of the castle walls.

They stopped in the town square and a mob of Castle Guard members spilled out after them with their swords drawn. The guards stopped in their tracks when they saw that the ones they were chasing now stood and faced them. They were not alone either. Behind David, his family, and friends were the entire city and members of rebel armies from across the country.

Valstayne shouted orders as he fought to make his way through the guards frozen in their tracks. He did not seem deterred by the backdrop of people behind his targets.

"Seize them!"

"I don't think our friends would let that happen," David objected.

"What makes you think my guards won't kill anyone who tries to stop me, boy?"

"What makes you think they want to fight their own friends and family?" Hannah responded.

The guards shifted their feet uneasily.

Sensing a change in their allegiance, Lord Valstayne turned to one of the guards, took his sword, and pointed it at David. "Then I will end this."

Before David could realize what was happening, Valstayne rushed at him. David reached for his sword, but it was no longer at his waist. Losing no time, George had already taken the sword from David and broke Valstayne's blow that was meant for his son.

"There is no need for another bloody battle," George tried to reason.

"Oh, I really think there is," Valstayne objected.

"Then, I call on an ancient tradition," George said.

"You want to invoke a one-on-one combat? You've been away from a sword too long."

"Then why are you sweating? Leader versus leader, me versus you, winner takes all."

"So be it," Valstayne agreed.

Instead of setting the rules and limitations as was custom, Valstayne just started swinging his blade. The crowd drew back to a safe distance and formed a circle around the fighting pair. Valstayne's constant attack kept George on the defensive, walking backward and never making the first move.

After three quick misses from Valstayne, George stepped forward and smashed the hilt of the sword into Valstayne's exposed shoulder blade. It knocked Valstayne off balance, and he had to take a few seconds to regain his footing. The pair was back on equal playing fields. Strikes and blows were met with skill. David was impressed that his father had not lost any of his talents over the years, but maybe Ethelrod brought out the best of these abilities in George when needed.

Valstayne made to strike horizontally when George decided to pull out a surprise move. George ran toward the blow, but at the last minute he slid on his knees below the sword and struck Valstayne's hamstrings with his own blade. George stood up and Valstayne crashed to the ground, dropping his sword in pain. David's father looked down at Lord Valstayne and held the tip of his sword to his opponent's throat. "Yield?" George asked.

Lord Valstayne held up his hands.

This was met with a cheering from the crowd on both sides. The country could finally start on the path toward peace.

George walked over to David and handed him the sword. "I think this belongs to you," George said with a wink. David took the sword with a smile, but he did not sheath it just yet.

George went to Lord Valstayne and honorably offered a hand to help him up. Valstayne accepted with his right hand, but suddenly David noticed a glint of metal in Valstayne's left hand.

"Dad!" David shouted.

Valstayne pulled out a dagger from his boot and pulled George in closer to his deadly weapon. Thanks to David's warning, George deflected the attack by grabbing Valstayne's wrist. With a swift movement, George flipped Valstayne head over heels until he landed back on the cobblestone street with a horrible sound. Red liquid flowed through the cracks of the stones underneath their feet. George rolled his opponent onto his back to reveal that Lord Valstayne had fallen on his own blade and was dead.

Elizabeth rushed to her husband and locked him in a firm embrace. David joined his parents.

It was all over.

"David," Hannah called. David turned to look at the girl he had brought into this mess. Even after all they had both been through, especially Hannah, she still looked beautiful. This time David made the first move, as he grabbed her by the waist and pulled her lips to his. This was happiness.

"Okay, okay," Mr. Linden joked.

Morgana held up her hand, and the crowd silenced.

"I, Morgana," she began, "of the house of stewards of Ethelrod, do declare that George and Elizabeth Wilson of the House of Faraman are the true and rightful heirs to the throne. I hereby stand down and hand power back over to the true rulers." Morgana knelt down, and everyone around followed suit including Gretchen and Garrett. David thought it was an amazing sight to see everyone before them on their knees.

Elizabeth looked a little nervous and uncomfortable, but George was glowing to be back where he knew he should truly be. He grasped Elizabeth's hand and held it up into the air. The entire crowd stood up and cheered.

"Well," Mr. Linden said to Hannah, "I think it's about time to be getting home."

"What?" Gretchen interrupted. "And miss the wedding?"

David quickly looked back and forth between Gretchen and Garrett's faces. They weren't kidding.

"All right!"

Chapter Thirty

In just a few short days, Gretchen and Garrett were husband and wife. It was a lovely ceremony held at the convent of the Ladies of the Veil, which it just so happens was where Mr. Linden had hidden his book. Guests were present from all over Ethelrod. George and Elizabeth were there as guests of honor, of course, being the new king and queen. Their families from the Western Shore were there, as was Sir Andrew, who was healing nicely with the help of a medicine man. It was a joyous occasion and one where it was announced that Gretchen and Garrett would be going on a trip.

"To the Southern Plains?" David asked confused. "But why?"

"We have both been through so much," Gretchen explained.

"We need a new start," Garrett finished.

"But the Southern Plains," David tried to understand. "I thought they were never ending. I thought those who searched to the end never came back."

"It's true," Garrett agreed.

"But David," Gretchen continued, "it is also said that those who travel to the edge of the Southern Plains never come back because the paradise they find is so beautiful that there is no need to return."

"After all this, we are going to try to find our paradise together," Garrett said.

In an odd way, David understood. "I know you will find it."

"I found that sword, didn't I?" Garrett motioned to the sword at David's waist.

"Don't you mean the shield?" David asked.

Garrett shifted his stance. "Ah, no," he explained. "Did you ever wonder what my original contest was? The one that got me a spot in the Castle Guard?"

"You said it was a story for another time," David remembered. "All I know is that you had a contest around the same time I did."

"Pretty much exactly the same time," Garrett replied. "Morgana's father had decided to throw a festival. As part of the festival, there would be a joust whose winner would win the best sword man had to offer. There was a call for all of the best blacksmiths to create the best sword, and my father was one of those blacksmiths. The creator of such a sword would get one free wish to be granted by the king."

"Which you won and asked to be a part of the Castle Guard," David reasoned.

"You know I always wanted a life of adventure."

"But what about this sword?"

"Well, being a young foolish child, I believed an old man's tale about a treasure-seeker's hoard in the Northern Mountains. It was easier than it seemed. I found your sword in a random cave and left."

"But Azreal—"

"I must be the thief he mentioned that caused him to go on such careful guard. I didn't believe in treasure-seekers because I had never seen one until a few days ago."

"And my sword?"

"Well, you and Gretchen kind of ruined the whole festival thing by showing up right before the first contest. But the king didn't mind, as there was still going to be a fight. The sword I presented to win my contest became the sword you fought with to win yours."

"Amazing!"

"You see," Garrett said, "it seems our paths were crossed from the start. Way before we even knew each other and became friends."

"I'm glad they did. None of this would have been possible without you." David motioned to Gretchen. "Both of you. I hope you find what you're looking for."

A woman walked up to Elizabeth after the wedding and was clearly very excited about something.

"Look, Your Majesty," she announced, as she pulled the edges of the skirt of her dress to reveal that it had not one opening in the fabric, but two, one for each leg. "Now you can wear a fine dress and ride your horse as you wish!"

David stared at the woman and tried not to laugh. "Culottes! Did she just invent culottes in Ethelrod?" Now he was noticeably giggling, but thankfully the woman had already walked away.

"David, this is big," Mr. Linden said. "Elizabeth, from the centuries since you left to when you have returned, how many changes or advancements have you noticed?"

"None, Tom," she replied.

"And now that you are back, things are moving forward."

"It's just culottes," David stated.

"It's not just culottes," Mr. Linden answered.

The look on his mother's face showed that she knew what Mr. Linden meant.

What does he mean they aren't just culottes?

Then it hit him.

Oh. True progress in Ethelrod relies on their presence. My parents have to stay in Ethelrod.

Do I?

That became the big question. George and Elizabeth were now in charge of bringing peace and progress to an entire land. They would need help. They would also need someone to carry on their legacy after they were gone. David felt he had to stay, but what staying in Ethelrod meant was painful.

Staying in Ethelrod meant giving up the former dreams he had of becoming a doctor or anything for that matter. It meant giving up an entire way of life. No cars, no electronics, no technology. No movie theaters, no malls. David would never see his friends again. He had to give up those relationships. But worst of all, he had to give up Hannah.

Hannah and David had spent almost every waking hour together since they were reunited. It was clear how strongly they felt for each other, which was why they both had a few tears in their eyes as Mr. Linden was preparing to go with his glowing book in his hands.

"I will never forget you," Hannah promised.

"I will always keep a little of you with me," David said.

They stepped away from each other, toward their parents. George and Elizabeth stood behind David in the Great Hall.

"You ready?" Mr. Linden asked. Hannah wiped some tears away and nodded. "Hold on tight. I don't want to leave you behind." Hannah grabbed onto his arm and held tight.

George looked over to his wife. "Do you think you can do it?"

Elizabeth looked away for a second and turned back. "I think I can."

"Do you think you can do it, Tom?" George asked.

What are they talking about? David wondered.

George repeated to Mr. Linden, "Do you think you can do it, Tom? Be the man we need?"

"Yes."

Mr. Linden started to slowly force the book closed, and the pages glowed.

George leaned forward and whispered in David's ear. "David, I believe you have great potential, but your future lies outside of this world. You need to be able to make your own destiny."

David was confused. "What?"

Elizabeth placed her hand on David's shoulder and squeezed as she whispered, "We love you, David. Remember that."

David had no idea what was going on with his parents. He kept looking forward and couldn't break his eyes away from the burning brilliant light of the pages as Mr. Linden was so close to closing the book. He was mesmerized.

Next, David felt his father's hand on his back and felt a huge amount of pressure as George forced David to topple forward toward Mr. Linden. David quickly reached out to break his fall and grabbed onto Mr. Linden's leg to stop himself.

Mr. Linden closed the book.

The next thing David knew, he was back in the library with Hannah and Mr. Linden.

"Where are my parents?" David demanded to know. "Where are they?" David spun around from his place on the floor hoping to find his parents behind him.

Was that what my parents were whispering about? Did they really just make this huge decision without me? Did this mean I will never see them again?

David was home. In that he felt strange relief.

David was without a family. That would take time to sink in. He felt alone.

Hannah was now on the floor with him.

"I'm sorry, David."

"David," Mr. Linden answered, "they are not here. It was a hard decision to send you home without them so that they can fulfill their duties in Ethelrod while giving you a chance at a normal life. It was the responsible choice."

"A normal life," David sneered. "Living without my parents because they chose to rule a fantasy kingdom without me is so normal. Look, I get it! They just really should have talked to me first. I might have understood if they explained it to me."

David stopped.

"Can we go back?" he asked.

Mr. Linden didn't answer immediately.

"Can we go back?" he asked again. "Can my parents come home?"

"Most likely the red book will still work," Mr. Linden started.

The ideas were flowing. "Then we can—"

"But it is doubtful the red book will take us back to Ethelrod now that the adventure has come to a close," Mr. Linden said.

"Then it's hopeless," David said, defeated.

Hannah was quiet for a moment. "Dad, isn't there anything we can do?"

"Well, there is a chance to see your parents again, David," he explained.

"What do you mean? You said the red book—"

"There is a slight chance that the story isn't over, but most likely the red book will not be any help to us anymore."

David didn't think this was good news.

"But," Mr. Linden continued, "there are others. I told your parents about them before they made their decision to send you back alone."

"Others?" This was great news!

"It was crucial that your parents stay in Ethelrod to complete their destiny, but it is possible that one of these other books might have the power to bring them back. Then again, they may not, but it's worth a try."

More books?

Where are they?

How can we find them?
What powers do these books have?

All of these questions and more raced through David's mind. Out of all these thoughts, though, only one was powerful enough to be verbalized.

"Then let's find these other books."

𝕬lexander 𝕯avidson is an author, secondary educator, and certified reading specialist with a BA from the University of Michigan and an MAT in Literacy Education from Madonna University. He has been a member of the National Council of Teachers of English since 2011 and has presented at the National Conference for Peer Tutoring in Writing and the Michigan Reading Association Annual Conference. While teaching reading and writing to middle school and high school students, Alexander strives to create written works that will interest his students and teach them valuable lessons at the same time.

For more information, please visit AlexanderDavidsonBooks.com.

The Visitor's Choice: A Search to Make Things Right
Questions and Topics for Discussion

• At the beginning of the novel, David has no choice but to trust Gretchen, a complete stranger, to help him. Given this situation, or a situation like this, would you have trusted Gretchen or continued on your own? What qualities should a person have for you to trust him or her?

• The author chose not to reveal how David traveled to Ethelrod until Chapter Six. Why do you think the author chose to do this? What effect did it have on your interpretation of the story?

• Describe the changes in David's character from the beginning of the book to the end.

• Why do you think David's opinion of reading changed throughout the novel? What is so valuable about the act of reading or being able to talk about reading with others?

• Princess Morgana tells David, "Just because something is tough or difficult, it doesn't mean that it isn't possible" (pg. 32). What does this mean? Can you name an obstacle that you have overcome? What helped you to achieve your goal? Explain.

• Princess Morgana also tells David, "Don't be afraid of a challenge when it can make you a better person in the end" (pg. 32). Do you agree with this statement? Describe an example of a challenge you experienced that made you a better person in some way.

• First Princess Morgana's marriage was out of her hands and then she was being manipulated by Lord Valstayne. Can you relate to Princess Morgana's desire to live her own life? What kind of pressures could someone have in their life today to make them wish for more freedom or control?

• Hannah Linden told David her reasons for running away from home. Why do you think she decided to come back? What did she hope to accomplish by returning home?

• When Hannah travels to Ethelrod with David, at first she wants to sit tight and do nothing. David convinces her otherwise. How can choosing not to act have just as much of an effect on the outcome as taking action? What effects could there be?

• There are a lot of choices being made in this novel by several main characters. David chooses to save Riordan and not marry the princess. George decides it's time to return to Ethelrod. Elizabeth decides to trade her family's fish necklace. Morgana trusts Valstayne's decisions. Gretchen and Garrett decide to help their new friend David. Choose one of these, or another important choice, and describe the consequences, planned and unplanned, that came with it.

• Why was Garrett not loyal to Valstayne? What does it mean to be loyal?

• Why do you think Gretchen and Garrett decided to take a risk and search for the end of the Southern Plains? Have you ever taken a risk that turned out to be good for you? Have you ever taken a risk that ended up being not so good?

• At the end of the novel, George and Elizabeth make an important choice about David's future. What do you think of their choice? Why do you think they chose to do this? Have you ever had to make a hard choice that would affect someone else's life? What would you do if you could never see your family again?

• David is only a high school student when visiting the land of Ethelrod. Why do you think he takes so much responsibility to help others he has only just met? What are the character traits that David has that make him so responsible?

• At a young age, David is in charge of making some major decisions in this novel. What would you do if you suddenly had to be this responsible and make all of the decisions? What are some moments from history when children were treated and relied on as adults?

• David uses a non-violent loophole to win his first tournament in Ethelrod. Sheriff Lustris and Lord Valstayne end up destroying themselves. The Wilsons have to solve a puzzle instead of slay a dragon to get their shield. Why do you think the author chose to have David, his friends, and family overcome their challenges in this way?

• Who is Lord Valstayne? What was his agenda? What was he willing to do to get power? Who do you know in our world today that you could compare him to?

• The subtitle of this novel is "A Search to Make Things Right." Have you ever made a mistake or done something wrong that you tried to fix? What did you do and how did you fix it?

• Do you think David and his friends will find the other books? Make a prediction.

• Similar to Thomas from James Dashner's *The Maze Runner,* David arrives in a place he knows nothing about, full of people he has never met. How would you react if you woke up in a similar situation? What is the first thing you would do?

• Similar to Harry Potter from J. K. Rowling's *Harry Potter and the Sorcerer's Stone,* David finds out that he is not who he thinks he is. His family is also no longer what he thought it appeared to be. What does it mean to have an identity? What factors from your life are important in creating your identity and who you are today?

• Similar to the Pevensie children from C. S. Lewis's *The Chronicles of Narnia,* David finds himself able to travel between worlds. Where would you travel if you had the power to travel anywhere in the world? Would you ever want to travel to an imaginary location? Describe that place you imagine.

~ More Praise for *The Visitor's Choice* ~

"This book is fast-paced and easy to follow, allowing for most readers to comprehend. Interesting at every twist and turn of the plot, leaving readers unable to put down. It's great for me and my friends because the characters are relatable and deep, keeping our interest in understanding them, as well as the plot."
~Kyler C., Age 14

"*The Visitor's Choice* is an engaging story that is exciting while encouraging thought at the same time. It is sure to hit its mark and encourage young readers to begin a lifetime of literacy!"
~Daniel Spilker, Director, Perdo Arrupe Learning Center, University of Detroit Jesuit High School and Academy

"A fun story to read, where the characters and events come alive in your mind with clarity and depth. This richly written story hits the mark with middle school boys. Their families will enjoy it, too." ~Geoffrey Sale, Father of three

"I think this would be a great book for my friends and me because it is full of adventure and creativity. It emphasizes the importance of books and how we truly can be transported into different worlds just from reading. I think this will remind everyone how special it is to be immersed in books and the interesting stories they tell." ~Lindsay W., Age 16

"I have enjoyed this book greatly. When I put it down, I couldn't wait for the next chance to read it again. I think kids will love this book because of all of the adventure and action. When I thought the story was going one way, it completely changed on me so I always found a new surprise. This book was very good."
~Peter L., Age 13